Spoils

Also by Tammar Stein
Kindred
High Dive
Light Years

Spoils

Tammar Stein

Alfred A. Knopf
New York

Text copyright © 2013 by Tammar Stein
Jacket art copyright © 2013 by Kamil Vojnar

Visit us on the Web! randomhouse.com/teens
Educators and librarians, for a variety of teaching tools,
visit us at RHTeachersLibrarians.com

Library of Congress Cataloging-in-Publication Data
Stein, Tammar.
Spoils / Tammar Stein.—1st ed.
p.   cm.
Summary: When seventeen-year-old Leni finds out that her family won the lottery due to a deal her sister made with the devil, she is determined to set things right.
ISBN 978-0-375-87062-0 (trade) — ISBN 978-0-307-97431-0 (ebook)
[1. Family life—Fiction. 2. Lotteries—Fiction. 3. Wealth—Fiction. 4. Devil—Fiction.
5. Angels—Fiction. 6. Jews—United States—Fiction.
7. Saint Petersburg (Fla.)—Fiction.] I. Title.
PZ7.S821645Sp 2013 [Fic]—dc23 2012044759

The text of this book is set in 11.5-point Goudy.

Printed in the United States of America
December 2013
10 9 8 7 6 5 4 3 2 1
First Edition

To Florida: my kooky, spooky, astonishingly beautiful adopted home state. We got off to a rough start (let's both pretend that little episode with Tropical Storm Barry didn't happen), but after all these years together, I find that you've snuck your way into my heart like an invasive species—alligators, cement-eating termites, "harmless" water snakes, hurricanes and all. You're amazing.

Chapter One

My parents bought me a dolphin when I was twelve, but I made them take her back.

They led me through the backyard of our huge new house, my mom's hands over my eyes, my dad's hands on my shoulders leading me forward; then they stopped in front of the pool, threw their hands in the air, and yelled, "Surprise! She's yours!" That was during those first few heady years after the win when they were still figuring out what money could buy and what it shouldn't.

My breath caught as I watched the dolphin's sleek steel-gray body fly through the length of our pool. Something awful twisted in the pit of my stomach as I saw this powerful predator trapped in our silly man-made folly. Instead of the giddy, excited birthday girl they were expecting, my parents got a full-blown fit. Livid and horrified, I made them call the marine-animal rescue program to come get her. My parents had to talk fast to explain why they had a dolphin in their backyard pool. But since their call also came with an extremely generous donation for the future care of my dolphin, they never got in trouble, even though it was illegal to keep a dolphin in a home pool.

The rest of the afternoon could best be described as grim. While we waited for the rescue team to arrive, we sat on the patio overlooking the pool with my dolphin swimming in frantic circles like a moth trapped in a glass jar. I couldn't bring myself to eat my cake—shaped like a dolphin, covered in unappetizing bright-blue icing that was rapidly melting in the sun. A few hours later, the rescue team came and loaded the dolphin into a special carrier lined with a foam mattress fitted for the dolphin's body and sprayers to keep her sensitive skin from drying out.

Silently we watched the dolphin get carted away. I could feel my parents' disappointment and disapproval like a heavy weight. Even my brother and sister thought I was being ridiculously self-righteous. But it wasn't that I didn't want my own personal dolphin; I wanted to keep her so badly that I cried myself to sleep after she left.

I had posters of humpback whales and the Greenpeace ships that fought to save them like other girls my age had posters of movie stars. What ocean-crazy girl wouldn't adore swimming with her own pet dolphin? I could see why they had gotten confused.

I was only twelve but I knew she could never be mine. An

internal compass triggered an alarm that blared: *No! It would be evil to keep her.*

Which is how five years later, as soon as my sister bursts through the tea shop's front door, I immediately know something is very wrong. My internal clock is ringing like a bell. As soon as I see her face, the mad and terrified look in her eyes, I shiver and know something very bad has happened. Something that money can't fix.

As it turns out, I'm half-right.

Chapter Two

I finish brewing two citrus green teas for an older couple with a baby in one of those strange new strollers, when the door flies open and my sister enters her shop, Steeped. I almost don't recognize her. From my view behind the counter, Natasha's blood-red pashmina flutters behind her like a demon's wings. Natasha's trips to Tennessee to visit her ex-boyfriend, Emmett, never turn out well for any of us, but this expression frozen on her face, this level of anguish, is new.

The door swings shut with a sweet little tinkle as the silver bell dances on its string. So an entrance fit for slamming doors and a gong of doom makes do with the calm, Zen-like atmosphere of the shop. Natasha spares a quick glance around, her pale eyes taking in the merchandise on the shelves, the swept floors, the inviting groupings of chairs and small tables. For all her drama and unpredictability, Natasha is a fine and responsible business owner. But she's off her game. As she comes toward me, she brushes by the couple heading out with their drinks. They give her a funny look and exchange glances the way you do when you pass a crazy person; then they hurry out of the shop as if to get their baby away from danger. I gaze after them, wishing I could follow.

Natasha lifts the partition and steps behind the counter, the air around her oddly dark and heavy. Natasha is often intense, charming when it suits her, horrid when it doesn't. But whatever her mood is, it usually makes sense. This doesn't. There's something unreadable in her face. As she steps near me, I wrinkle my nose. Even the way she smells is off.

"Tasha," I say. "You okay?"

She ignores the question.

"Shop's been good?" she asks, her voice oddly raspy and subdued. She's been gone nearly two weeks, the longest she's been away since she opened the store almost five years ago.

"Yeah." I nod cautiously. "Pretty typical." When Natasha makes an impatient little motion for me to go on, I add, "There's a knitting group that wants to host their monthly meetings here. Thursday evenings. I said it was probably fine, but that I'd check with you."

She has a manager for the shop, a creep named John Parker, but she likes me to keep an eye on it while she's gone. I don't let Natasha pay me, though she's offered more than once. I like feeling like the shop is my second home, and you can't clock in and out for pay in your second home. You can, however, help yourself to tea and blueberry scones.

Natasha's annual buying trips usually finish with a visit to her ex in Tennessee, an old high school boyfriend and the only guy she's ever been in love with. After they broke up, she lent him the money to open his tattoo shop. Anyone else and it would be sweet, friendship after romance. Cynically, I saw it as less of a generous gesture than an iron-proof way to force him to answer to her. She wasn't visiting Emmett because her feelings mellowed into friendship. She went there for the same reason she lent him money in the first place, because she's never given up on getting him back.

As she makes her way around the counter, I expect her to brew up a pot of gunpowder tea and then go over the books, or review inventory, see what's running low and needs reordering. After she's gone, foul mood or no, she always wants to know every last detail of what she missed while she was gone.

Instead, she says, "Thanks, Leni," and then keeps going, through the beaded curtain to her small office in the back. Before I can ask how her trip was and figure out what's wrong, she shuts the door behind her with a firm click.

The air-conditioning kicks on and a cool breeze blows across my neck, making me squirm.

Half an hour later the office door's still closed. I press my ear against Natasha's shut door but there's nothing besides the flutes.

"Tasha? What's wrong?" I say to the wood-paneled door.

Silence. No answer.

"Natasha, what happened?" I try the handle but it's locked.

An inexplicable rush of dread comes over me. For a terrible second, when there is nothing, no reply, no sound at all, I think maybe she's dead. Which is ridiculous and I'm not one prone to crazy flights of imagination. But there was something so wrong about her, something broken.

I thump into the door with my shoulder, trying to force it open. It remains solidly closed. I rub my shoulder. There's still no sound coming from inside the room. Nothing. My irrational/rational fear grows, and everything I learned in that survival course from four years ago comes rushing back, along with a welcome shot of adrenaline. As I step into a fighting position, my muscles bunch, ready to explode with a powerful front kick aimed left of the locked handle. But then I hear rustling and stop myself in time, tripping forward a bit to stop the momentum.

"Natasha," I bellow, pounding the door and rattling the handle. "Let me in!"

There's more rustling and eventually the click of the lock. The ceramic handle turns under my hand. And there she is, small and haggard, blotchy skin with, I could swear, a tinge of green to it.

My sister is the beautiful one in the family, creamy white skin, long dark hair with deep glints of burgundy. My hair is lighter, bleached from too much time in the sun, my skin darker, tanned from hours spent kayaking on the bay. We have the same color eyes, greenish, bluish gray. On me they sort of blend in with whatever I'm standing next to, like a chameleon.

On Natasha, they glow. After she got the massive tattoo of a Japanese scroll across her back a few years ago, she only wore long, backless dresses, and coming or going she made you catch your breath.

She's taken off her red shawl and is wearing her signature backless dress, water-colored silk in blues and greens, except without her high heels the long skirt puddles around her feet and she looks like a child playing dress-up.

"Natasha," I say, confusion and worry mingling. "What happened?"

Her eyes pool with tears at the soft question. My sister never cries. Curses, screams in rage, laughs out loud, rolls her eyes, and shoots death-ray glares, yes. Pathetic weeping? Not so much. I shake my head as if to clear it.

Natasha's ex-boyfriend is a big guy. He's the one who did the tattoo, and he has been the object of her obsessive love since she was fifteen. I quickly scan her bare arms, the deep V of her dress, for bruises or marks. He never struck me as the violent type, but maybe Natasha's nine-year obsessive crush finally drove him over the edge.

"What did Emmett do to you?"

"It wasn't him." Her tears spill over. "He didn't do anything."

The silver bell hanging from the front door tinkles musically.

Steeped is perfectly located on a busy thoroughfare with a beautiful view of the bay, which means there's usually a steady stream of customers. We were lucky to have ten minutes without interruption. I glance over my shoulder through the beaded curtain. There's a guy studying the giant menu over the counter.

8

"Be right with you," I call. Then I give Natasha a stern look. "Wash your face. Then tell me what the heck happened to you." She flinches at my tone but turns and slowly makes her way to the restrooms.

I hurry to the customer, in his midthirties with funky purple wire glasses and auburn highlights. He asks about our chai; we carry three kinds.

"They're all good." I keep listening for Natasha, expecting her to pop back out, take charge like she always does. "It depends what you're in the mood for." Seeing that this isn't going to speed things along, I interrupt his internal debate. "I prefer the Indian masala chai. We ship it directly from India. We're the first tea shop in America to carry this blend."

That little speech always seals the deal and sure enough, I'm soon brewing an order of Indian masala chai.

Before I can head back to crisis-manage my sister, a couple of girls my age walk in. One looks familiar and when she keeps looking at me, I know with a sinking feeling that we must have gone to school together.

My parents used to send me to the fanciest, most expensive school in St. Petersburg. That was actually how they made their decision. They looked at the tuition of all the private schools in the area and chose the highest one.

I hated St. John's. I hated the brand-new cars in the parking lot, the five-hundred-dollar purses the girls carried, the expensive haircuts. I even hated the teachers, with their eager faces, their anxious desire for their students to succeed and to like them. So after I overheard my parents argue about money, the first such fight in five years, I quietly applied to South St. Pete's

Citrus Park High, the science magnet high school, known for its terrific marine-science program and ghetto location. Once I was accepted, I came to my parents and begged to switch.

I should have realized that things were getting bad, and fast, when with very little begging and pleading on my part, my parents let me transfer and attend a school at the edge of one of the worst neighborhoods in the city, where a little girl had died in a drive-by shooting a few months earlier and two policemen were killed in the line of duty a couple of years back.

I don't regret switching schools but it's never fun bumping into former St. John's schoolmates. Somehow, they always manage to convey that by leaving the school to go to a public high school, I was no longer "one of them." These two are no different. After an awkward little visit down not-so-fond memory lane, I take their order, serve them and send them on their way.

The moment they're out the door, I hurry to my sister's office. Her back is to me, head resting on her folded arms at her desk. She's usually very aware of her tattoo, of her body, and like a model she always makes sure she's displayed in the best light, at the best angle. In this position, though, Natasha's curved spine puts the tattoo in stark relief, the Japanese characters stretched out. It's not a good pose for her.

A horrible thought occurs to me.

"Natasha, are you pregnant?"

"What?" Her head snaps back to stare at me. "Don't be an idiot."

I let out a breath I wasn't aware I was holding. Natasha procreating. I shudder. The world is not ready.

"Leni," she says, her voice cracking. "You can't even imag-

ine, you can't . . ." She loses her train of thought and her eyes focus on something over my shoulder. Instinctively, I look behind me, but there is nothing there.

"Your birthday's coming up," she says suddenly.

"Yeah," I say, wary about this change of topic. "The big one-eight."

My birthday is in nine days and Natasha has already offered the shop to host the party. The gala, as my parents keep calling it. It's a joke of epic proportions to think of hosting a gala for my eighteenth birthday. It's only with the free use of space and Natasha's wholesale contacts that it's even conceivable, and even so it seems like a colossal waste of money. I told my parents that I would rather they tally up how much they were planning to spend and make a donation in my name to a couple of organizations that work to protect Tampa Bay, but they laughed me off and said they'd do both.

Maybe Natasha's reneging on hosting the party. Fine by me.

"Don't give the money to Mom and Dad," she says.

"Whoa." I hold up my hands. "Where the hell did that come from?"

"Watch your mouth," she snarls at me.

"What is your problem, Natasha?" I snap back.

"Do us all a favor, okay?" she says. "Get rid of the money. As soon as you can. As soon as you turn eighteen. Get rid of it. Give it away. Burn it. I don't care. But it's got to leave our family." She chews on her thumbnail, a bad habit she broke years ago. It's only because of how off she looks, how shattered, that I'm willing to go along with the change of subject.

"You're not there when the water's turned off and D

brings in buckets of water from the pool to flush the toilets. Okay? You don't have any right to tell me what to do with that money."

"Yeah, I do." Her knuckles turn nearly white as she clutches the edge of her desk. She almost looks frightened, except that makes no sense at all.

"Why are we even talking about this?" I ask, exasperated, trying not to raise my voice. "I don't have a choice. Mom and Dad are expecting that money. Let me rephrase. They're *counting* on that money. It's not mine to keep."

"Lenore," my sister says harshly, letting go of the desk and lurching forward, clutching my arm and stepping so close that our bodies nearly touch. She has to look up to meet my eyes. She's been wearing heels for so long, I never realized I'm taller. "That money is cursed." Her voice is low and hoarse as she enunciates. Her breath is sour in my face. "Get. Rid. Of. It."

First of all, I hate it when people call me Lenore. She knows that. Secondly, her sharp nails dig into the tender skin of my arm and the small hairs on my nape rise, that prehistoric response to danger.

"Natasha," I say, as if to a child. "It's just money. We can do whatever we want with it." I try pulling her fingers off.

"Listen to me." She tightens her grip. "It . . . it was rigged, okay? That's all I can tell you. We never should have won that money in the first place."

Okaaaay.

This argument, this fight, whatever this conversation is, has devolved into a farce.

12

"Excuse me?" I ask, as if checking she's still there. My sister has never had troubles with reality, with sanity, but Mom has an aunt that was institutionalized. "Are you on something? You're not making any sense. And you're freaking me out."

"Leni." She takes a shaky breath, visibly fighting for calm. "I know this sounds insane. I know you don't believe me. But I'm telling the truth. The only reason Dad won the lottery was because of me, because I made a deal." She lets go of my arm and uses her hands to rub her face, like she's trying to wake up. "A really, really bad deal." She covers her face, hiding her naked emotions as she starts crying.

I let her cry for a bit as I follow the logic.

Logically, I don't see how what my sister is saying could be true. It's not possible to rig the lotto; they have insane safeguards to make sure of that. Even assuming that it was somehow true, who could Natasha have possibly known who would do that for her when she was in high school?

"Tasha," I say, asking the third thing about this that doesn't make any sense. "Why would you even want to win the lottery badly enough to mess with some badass hacker people? Our life was fine."

"I thought Emmett would stay if I was rich. So stupid." Her voice cracks. Long black streaks of eyeliner and mascara have turned her face into a gruesome mask. "I was so stupid."

Out of Natasha's whole ridiculous story, that's one thing that rings true. Natasha would have done *anything* to keep Emmett. She was never good with boundaries, and when she fell in love with him in high school and they started dating, nothing he ever gave her was enough. She didn't want him to spend a second without her. Emmett put up with Natasha's craziness longer than a lot of guys would but when he graduated, he enlisted in the army. Natasha almost went insane. He was going to leave her, leave St. Pete, and who knew when or if he'd ever be back. I barely saw her during that period. I was a tomboyish ten-year-old, obsessed with marine biology, out on the beach every second I could be. It wasn't until I was fifteen and in the midst of an ugly breakup with my first boyfriend that I even thought about how painful and heartbreaking it was to have someone you love say "no thank you." But it never occurred to me to question the timing of winning the lottery and Natasha's bad breakup.

"A deal works both ways," I say, pretending this is real, pretending what she said could be true. "What did you promise?"

"I promised that I would do what he asked," she says, taking a shaky breath. "One thing. Whenever he asked it." She swipes at her cheeks, smearing the black lines across her face. It is surreal to see my perfect sister ruined with tears and paint.

"That's pretty open-ended," I say. What could she possibly do for a Mafia hacker that was worth millions?

"I told him I wouldn't do anything that hurt our family or anyone we knew." She crosses her arms defensively.

"And when is . . . is . . ." It's hard to say it out loud. Like a joke. ". . . is this hacker person getting his one favor?"

"He just did," she says, her skin matching her dress as she swallows convulsively, greasy with a film of sweat. "He cashed in his chip this morning."

A nervous tremor runs through me despite my skepticism. "What did he want?"

"It's none of your business," my sister says in an empty voice. She turns away, returning to her earlier position, back to the door, hunched over her desk, her vertebrae jutting in a skeletal column through skin and indecipherable Japanese characters. "Get rid of that money, Leni."

I walk over and place a hand on her back. Her skin is oddly chilled and clammy.

"Natasha, what hap—"

"Get rid of it, Lenore," she snaps as she turns to me, her spittle flying and hitting my face. I stumble back. "It's got blood on it." She touches a hand to her lips, as if to take back the words, but I see the truth in her eyes.

"Natasha," I whisper. "What did you do?"

But she won't say anything else.

As they left the shop behind, she couldn't shake off the uneasy feeling lurking heavy in her chest. She checked on the baby, lifting the canopy for a quick peek, to see that sweet little sleeping face again. To make sure she was okay.

Motherhood had had all sorts of surprises for her. The fierce mama-bear love, the constant need to see the baby, to hold her, to feel her tiny chest rising and falling, was a huge one. Sometimes she would slip out of bed at night and creep down the hall, only to ease down silently next to the crib and watch the baby in the dim light from the blue-moon night-light.

She glanced at Craig: husband, father, laid-off accountant.

He wore his now-familiar look of stress and worry. Everything had happened together. The baby was born and a month later, Craig was out of a job. They had said it was a blessing; he could spend this time with his new daughter. So many fathers didn't. They figured he'd find something within a couple of months, and it was wonderful to have another set of hands when spit-up came out of one end while the other end squirted impossibly foul matter and the baby screamed like someone was performing surgery without anesthesia on her. They'd laughed in drunken, sleep-deprived jags, going through baby boot-camp together, and she'd pitied other couples who missed out on this. Gazing over their sleeping newborn together, melting over those fleeting, toothless sleep-smiles.

Except the weeks turned to months and there were no interviews, no job offers. Craig began applying for jobs below his previous level, willing to take salary cuts. And still, no job offers. It wasn't about them anymore. They were parents now. It left her with a hollow feeling of panic. What kind of parents can't provide for their child? Even though they'd agreed she'd stay at home for at least a year, she started submitting her résumé, not that she had any better luck. They even discussed moving in with his parents, just until one of them found a job. When they drove by the Powerball billboard and saw someone had won the jackpot, both of them couldn't help thinking how much they could have used that money. It was hard to stop the daydreams about how they could use that money.

Fantasy aside, they needed to decide what they were going to do. But all she could think about was that woman who had come into the tea shop after them. She shivered again, though the day was blazing hot.

"She was weird, right?" she said.

And Craig, bless him, knew exactly what she meant.

"Yeah," he said. "Freaky."

"She really scared me. When I see people like that, I get scared that they want to hurt Libby." She shivered again, feeling so off-kilter she had to stop and peek through the sun visor on the stroller to check on the baby again, as if some evil spirit could have snuck into her little carrier and spirited her away.

"We would never let anything bad happen to her," Craig said firmly, her practical and pragmatic sweetie.

They were silent after that, he pushing the stroller, she walking at his side, both taking occasional sips of their teas. They walked all the way to the pier and then to its end, where Tampa Bay stretched out and the fishermen fished with their endless patience.

"We have to let the house go, don't we?" she finally said, leaning against the railing, her back to the million-dollar view as she looked at her husband and daughter.

"Yeah," he said. "We do."

"And then it's off to Illinois. And your parents."

"Yeah. At least, for a little while."

She felt an aching sadness at the thought of leaving their bungalow with its beautiful views and happy memories. But it was the right decision. They were parents now.

"I love you," she said, and leaned over to him, touching her lips very gently to his cheek. "And Libby is lucky to have you for a daddy."

Craig smiled, his eyes sad and sweet. "Right back at you." They hugged each other, leaning into each other's strength.

Then Libby woke up, hot and fussy, and soon they were busy changing a soiled diaper and fixing a bottle, and then the heat was too much. They pitched their drinks into the trash and headed home.

Chapter Three

Natasha refuses to answer any questions. She cleans up and paints her face back on, though she still looks forlorn and haunted behind the counter. I hurry out into the bright, punishing heat, leaving the dark shop behind like a bad dream.

We have electricity and running water at home this month, but still the house is an awful, depressing place that I'm in no hurry to return to. The quiet headache I've been ignoring all day has sharpened. Wicked pain drills through my right eye and I squint against the sharp brightness of a Florida afternoon. It's difficult to credit the things Natasha has told me, not because she's a liar, it's just impossible to believe. And it's Natasha.

My mom says that the three of us were born with our personalities fully in place.

My older brother, Eddie, was born tired. "Born tired and lives to sleep," my mom always says. It was three days until she knew the color of his eyes, because he wouldn't open them. He even fed with his eyes closed.

Natasha was born screaming. She didn't stop for five months. My parents thought she had colic, but it was just Natasha letting everyone know she was here and pissed off about it. When she was young, our acquaintances thought she was the sweetest little girl, though really what they meant was that she was cute and pretty. My mom would get compliments about her adorable girl at the mall and the grocery store. Babysitters, on the other hand, hated watching her. It was hard to find one who'd come back a second time. Natasha was a biter.

As for me, according to my mom, I was born with an old soul. I had big, solemn eyes. I rarely cried and my mom said that I stared at her like I was trying to figure everything out, like I was trying to read her thoughts. I learned to talk earlier than either my brother or sister, and my first word, at nine months, was "ish," which meant fish. Every morning I would wake up and shout from my crib, "Ish! Ish!" My favorite thing to do was to go to the pier and look at the fish.

So maybe my mom's right. There's Eddie, back at the house, twenty-seven, unemployed and probably buzzed even though it's barely four in the afternoon. Natasha at the tea shop, too thin, strung too tight, saying those crazy things. And me, still obsessed with fish, still trying to figure everything out.

Nothing changes.

But that's not true, because things did change for our family. After we won the lottery, everything changed.

At Lenny's Restaurant, my favorite breakfast place, the ceiling tiles are painted with all sorts of funny sayings. One that always makes people snort is: *Lord, help me prove to you that I can win the lotto and stay humble.* They also post the winning lottery numbers next to their Sunday-morning specials. It's cute. People dream about winning the lottery and how it'll change their lives. The fact that the change will be for the better is taken for granted. Since when did copious, ridiculous, Monopoly amounts of money not fix everything? No more fretting about that tight race between the checking-account balance and the bills in the mail. No more envious longing for someone else's cool crap. Being rich is like being famous without the stalking paparazzi. It means you're important and powerful. Of course that's a better life. Of course you'd be a happier person. Duh.

But the thing is, after the shock, after the giddy dizziness fades, after you wake up and the money is still there and after you finally come to believe that this isn't the most vivid, amazing dream you've ever had, that this is real—after all that, you're still you. There are still traffic jams. You still get bored. You get pissed when people are rude and thoughtless. You barely miss being in a horrible crash when some texting idiot runs a red. You have bad morning breath and pimples. None of your friends are millionaires, and suddenly you're this weird creature, an evolutionary mutant with no genus to belong to. Within a year, our friends split into two basic groups: those who were jealous of us and those who were uncomfortable and awkward around us. And that was the problem, really. Once we won, the money didn't change who we were, it changed how people saw us. And once that happened, nothing made the sense it used to.

When I was eight, two years before we won, my siblings and I pooled our money and together with help from my dad, we bought my mom a Le Creuset pot for Mother's Day. She'd wanted one for years. Not a cheaper knockoff you could find at T.J.Maxx. She always wanted the real thing from France, but at the same time, she felt it was ridiculous to spend $150 on a pot, even a brightly colored, guaranteed-to-cook-amazing-dinners, enameled cast-iron pot.

On that Mother's Day, we drove to the Ellenton Premium Outlets and found her a cerulean-blue Dutch oven on sale at the Le Creuset outlet.

My mom loved that pot. Every time she used it, she made a point to say something about her adorable children buying it for her. She loved to carry it to the table, set it down and lift the lid like a magician presenting a delightful surprise. The fragrant steam, curling with promise, always backed her up.

A couple of months after we won, when I was almost eleven, my mom picked me up from school and said, "Let's go!"

We drove to the Williams-Sonoma in Tampa's Old Hyde Park Village, a posh shopping district. My mom was in the grips of this weird joy. There was nothing in that fancy store that we couldn't buy. We didn't need to wait for a sale. We didn't need to drive to the outlet. We didn't need to compromise on color or shape or choose only one. The salesladies picked up on the energy like a contact high. We were all giggling.

My mom ended up buying every type of Le Creuset they had in stock: the braiser, the stockpot, the gratin dish, all of it. A saleslady talked her into buying a complete set of silicone cooking utensils, a red stand mixer and a doughnut maker. I begged for a cake mold in the shape of a giant cupcake. The total bill was close to $4,000.

We needed help carrying it all to our car, and they tromped along to our brand-new Lexus SUV, a little parade of happy consumers. We were giddy from the power, the potential, the promise of all the good times to come. We could buy it all.

Then we got home and unloaded the boxes. They piled higher and higher on our little kitchen counters. We hadn't built the new house yet. There was nowhere to put all the new cookware, so we ended up storing it in the garage. A tower of bright orange boxes next to the old TV, computer boxes and sound system that took up most of the space our car used to park in.

She never used the doughnut maker and we tried out the giant cupcake mold once, but really, who wants to eat a giant, cake-sized cupcake? The Le Creusets she liked but she hardly used most of them. Her favorite was still the blue one we got on sale for Mother's Day. Her first Le Creuset, the one her children bought for her.

Because it turns out you can't buy more of that feeling you get when the people you love show you how much they love you back. Not even at Williams-Sonoma for $4,000. That's what winning the lotto felt like. A big initial thrill, followed by the dawning realization that most of its promises were hollow.

Then, over the course of seven insane years, even the hollow promises were gone. There was no money left. Except for my trust fund, which matures next week.

* * *

I come to my favorite part of the St. Pete bay walk, a bend
that turns in to make a little nook with a couple of palm trees
shading the cove from the sun. I lock my bike and hop down
to the sand. The impact jostles my headache, making it flare
into bursts of lightning crackling behind my eyes and temples.
A migraine. I haven't had one since leaving St. John's. Tuck-
ing my hair behind my ears, I ease down, settling in with my
back against the seawall to watch the waves and the birds and
anything that might swim by. With a light breeze off the water,
it's fifteen degrees cooler in the shade.

When I leave for college next year, I won't be able to see the
water every day, something I can't imagine. My dream school
is Stanford. Forty-thousand-dollars-a-year Stanford. I want to
study marine science, get a doctorate and do everything I can
to take care of the most amazing ecosystem in the world. Ten to
twelve years of higher education. My trust fund would go a long
way toward covering that.

I shift uncomfortably at the thought of the money. I try
not to think about it. I try not to think of it as *mine*. Because
if I start thinking about it that way, it'll be very hard to hand
it over to my parents and see them spend it on more crap. And
then there's Natasha's story about how we shouldn't have won
in the first place, messing me up even more. I shake my head,
as if plagued by mosquitoes. My headache pulses in protest and
I immediately stop.

Without even realizing it, I slip into my meditating position,
learned in one of the endless sets of classes my parents bought

for me. Slowly the soft breeze and the sound of the wavelets lapping at the shore work their usual magic. Two seagulls cry to each other. My foul, messed-up mood starts to smooth out. Because I'm tucked against the bottom of the seawall, walkers up on the sidewalk never notice me.

I take a deep breath and whoosh it out, clearing my mind of all thoughts and focusing on *om*, the sound of the vibrations of the universe. Tiny hypnotic waves come again and again and eventually my heart settles into that slow, slow beat and my muscles let go of some of the tension. The headache, while still there, starts feeling like something happening to another person. The worries, doubts and confusion melt away and I sink toward oblivion.

I'm in that lovely state, calm and centered, eyes closed, when the first blow hits me.

My head snaps back like I'm a stunt double being kicked in the face. I fly out of my lotus position, arms flailing, legs kicking out, and the back of my head hits the rough seawall behind me. Stars explode under my closed eyes, flashes of light. The migraine roars in fury. I'm in the most densely populated county in Florida, on a popular beach, but given my spot, no one will see me, no one will come to my aid. I have time to think that, to feel afraid, before the migraine intensifies. It grows from the inside out until my skull creaks under the pressure and there's no room for thoughts at all. I curl into a fetal position on the sand, arms clutching my head. A bombing-raid victim with no bomb shelter.

There's a high-pitched whimpering. It's coming from me.

Lenore, says a terrible voice. *Lenore!* It's so loud, people must hear it in Budapest. It's in my bones, rattling my teeth. It's in my throat, metallic and sharp.

I hold my breath, waiting for the next blow. It's coming. The pressure spikes, my ears pop, my heart races, the lizard part of my brain going nuts.

Fix it, the voice roars. It's deafening, furious, righteous and utterly confident.

Pain explodes in my temples and I arch back, screaming. My arm scrapes against the seawall but the burn is a faint echo, happening far away.

Fix it!

"I will!" The words rip from my throat, almost without my consent. "I will!"

I'll say anything to make the pain stop, to make the voice go away. It works. As soon as I pledge, the voice, the migraine, the pain and pressure all vanish. Disappearing like gigantic sea monsters sinking back into the deep, they leave the churning water to calm and sailors to shiver with primal terror. Terrible things still lurk below.

When I come back to myself, to consciousness, it's almost dark. I have been swimming up and up and up, from the deepest dive ever taken. Kicking up and up and up, straining to reach the surface, my lungs aching with the need to breathe. I wake with a gasp, gulping for air. I'm covered in a thin film of sand. I have been lying like this for hours.

My arm oozes blood from half a dozen sand-clogged scrapes, and there's a goose-egg-sized lump on the back of my head.

As I stand up slowly, the blood rushes in painful prickles to my numb legs.

I rub my head, remembering the horrible headache. There's nothing left of it, thank God, only a faint echo, a twinge that makes me cringe in memory.

I try to gather what I remember, though the strands are like slippery gossamer. I rub my forehead harder, as if to physically make my brain give up its secrets. Unbidden, tears well up. I wipe them away in disgust.

I am not a religious person; I've hardly ever been to synagogue. I've never even read the Bible. So there's no reason for the utter conviction, the bone-deep certainty, that the terrifying, agonizing encounter I've just had was with an angel. I even know his name. It shimmers in front of me, letters written in the dark with a glow stick: *michael*.

Holding a hand before me, I can almost keep it steady and my vision isn't blurry or split in two. It's not a concussion. I don't have dementia. I fight to hold on to reason, to logic, in the face of this irrational, illogical event.

I review the facts:

1. I meditated on the beach.
2. An angel spoke to me. (It was horrifying, painful, traumatic, but these are adjectives. I'm trying to stick with facts.)
3. I promised him something.

Q: Could this be a case of mistaken identity?

A: Unlikely.

Q: Is a promise given under duress (with zero explanation of what is expected) binding?

A: Probably. Given my luck lately, definitely.

Q: What did I promise to fix?

A: I don't know ... but maybe I do.

Q: And if I fail?

A: ...

The pain, the violence, the terrible ringing voice, they came from within. When I meditated and went deep inside, something rose up to meet me.

Michael.

When he disappeared, he didn't leave me. He only sank out of sight again. Which means that he knows what I know and sees what I see. If I fail him, he could rip me to pieces, from the inside out.

Chapter Four

With a last look at the bay, all dark and mysterious, I clamber up the wall, fully expecting to be accosted again. Surely, the angel knows I'm leaving the beach clueless. Freaked out, bleeding, but essentially clueless. Yet nothing stops me as I unlock my bike and set off for home.

With my shaky legs at the pedals and trembling hands at the handlebars, I watch the sky finish its evening dance, turning from blue to lavender to indigo, and as the light fades, the temperature drops along with it, coming down from the mid-nineties. Only the sidewalks still pulse with heat, a testament to the earlier scorcher. The landscape gradually changes from high-rise condominiums, shops and restaurants to large mansions separated by rolling lawns and high fences. Our stupid house isn't the largest of these monsters, but it's big enough. Knowing all the sand dunes and turtle-nesting sites that were flattened and paved over to build it makes me hate it even more. It's unnatural. The periodic hurricanes, blowing through like the sheriff evicting people from their foreclosed homes, prove it.

I push my bike over the uneven pavers to the massive front doors, carved in Germany. I unlock them, push the left one open and wheel my bike in, parking it in the white marble foyer. There used to be fresh flowers on the circular table in the entryway, delivered every three days. That was one of the first things my parents cut when they realized that the money was running out. They didn't think that much money could ever disappear. They thought they would be rich forever.

Without bothering to turn on any lights, I climb up the marble staircase, my hand trailing on the wrought-iron banister, the sound of my steps echoing up to the high ceiling, bouncing against the empty walls.

I wash my bloody arm in the bathroom and carefully pat it dry.

Entering my hideous room, I flop on the canopied bed, stare at the dusty canopy and try to come to terms with what happened.

The archangel Michael spoke to me.

I allow the thought to repeat. *Michael, an archangel, came to me while I was meditating.*

I wait to see what my mind will say about that.

Yes, it says back. *I know.*

I shiver as the downy hair on my arms and legs rises, a primordial reaction to appear bigger to a predator. I look at the blond, nearly invisible hair. Useless. Pathetic.

I press my feverish face into the cool pillows. Michael. The angel. Came to me while I was meditating and spoke to me. But the details are fuzzy. As time passes since the visit, the details fade. I scramble up and grab a sheet of paper out of the printer's paper tray on my desk, and scrawl the words that are still clear and ringing like a bell. The words that ripped out of my throat, the words that yanked me out of the meditation, out of the hellish place I'd landed in. Spoken out loud to the sand, the water, the salty air and to whatever, whoever was there with me that evening.

I'LL FIX IT.

I sit back and look at the words. *Okay,* I think. *Okay. I will.*

I fire up my computer and begin filling the massive gaps in my knowledge. There are thousands of site hits for the archangel Michael, but I stick to the main ones, looking for some basic information, a crash course in angelology.

Field commander of the army of God, says one site.

Guardian angel of Adam, says another.

Patron of humanity, insist several.

The goose egg on the back of my head and the throbbing from my right arm beg to differ.

The archangel Michael tried to protect the Jewish Temple from destruction, but the sins of the people were too great. This entry gives me pause. It's hard to imagine anything being beyond the powers of this angel. Not good. This is not good. Natasha's face swims before me. *The sins of the people were too great.*

For the first time since I meditated on the beach, I think back to my sister and our conversation in the tea shop. This can't be a coincidence. But seriously, an angel appearing because the lottery was rigged seven years ago? Doesn't make sense. Which is when I realize that whatever Natasha isn't telling me is big. And it's bad.

I come down for dinner later, feeling like a bell that has recently been rung; there's no sound anymore but if you touched it lightly, you'd feel the lingering vibrations tingle down your arm.

The Campbell-soup casserole fills the kitchen with a homey scent. The kitchen might be heavy with stainless steel, and professional-grade Viking appliances, but the cooking there hasn't changed much since the big win. Some things, even my parents felt, were fine to begin with. We might have eaten more steak and seafood than before, and even the sugar and the paper towels were organic for a little while, but my parents' basic tastes stayed the same. It was especially helpful when we started cutting back; cooking dinners at home was what we all preferred in the first place.

I help my mom finish the salad, full with my thoughts, turning them this way and that way, trying to see how they fit together. I set out the plates and silverware on the granite counter at the kitchen island, where we always eat. There's a massive oak table that can seat twenty in the dining room. We've used it twice in the last five years. Turns out that buying a big table doesn't mean you'll have the friends (or the grand parties) to fill it.

My mom looks at me inquiringly like she's been trying to get my attention for a while. My mom is the only one in the family with blue eyes and blond hair. As always, she's put together in a tidy, conservative way, Florida-style; today she's wearing sky-blue capris and a lime-green collared shirt, her hair in a neat pageboy.

"Natasha's back from Tennessee," I tell her. It's as good an excuse as any to explain my distraction. And of course, Natasha's return really must be responsible for the afternoon's events.

My mom grimaces comically. "How many cups did she break?"

Natasha keeps the chipped and cracked mugs from Steeped in her office so that she can smash them in fits of temper. It's that weirdly practical, crazy side of her that charms some people and drives others nuts.

I pause, not sure how much to tell my mom. "She didn't break anything." Something in my tone causes my mom to stop fixing the salad and look at me. "She just cried."

My mom's mouth forms an O of surprise.

"It was kind of pathetic," I say, "and creepy coming from Natasha."

"Maybe it means there was finally some sort of closure there. I always said Emmett wasn't doing her any kindness not cutting her off." My mom sighs. "I'll try to talk to her tonight."

I shake my head. "I think . . . I think she needs some alone time."

My mom and Natasha often use me as a sort of neutral intermediary. So now, when I give my mom advice on dealing with Natasha, she accepts that I speak as Natasha's representative.

"I had something really weird happen to me on the way home," I start. I feel a real pang of fear for my sister at the thought that what happened to me this afternoon is because of something she did. Belatedly I also realize that the rest of us are implicated in this mess too. We've all used the money. I swallow past the sudden lump in my throat.

My mom returns to chopping tomatoes for the salad, her quick knife skills a testament to the expensive knife she uses. My parents hired a personal chef when we first moved here, but that lasted less than a month. It wasn't as great as it sounds, having a stranger in the kitchen do all your cooking. Nothing ever turned out the way we thought it would. Nothing tasted quite right.

I hesitate now, thinking of all the money my family has spent the last seven years. How badly it's been wasted, the implications of that.

My mom makes a sort of *mmm* sound, encouraging me to continue. As I take a breath to try and explain what happened to me this afternoon, maybe even figure it out for myself, the phone rings, shrill and loud. My mother's hand slips.

"Damn it!" She clutches her thumb and looks at it in astonishment. The cut is so fine that at first there isn't any blood. "It doesn't even hurt."

By the time I wet a paper towel and hand it to her, the phone ringing insistently in the background, the blood has started gushing. She wraps the towel around her finger and hisses as the pain finally kicks in. Within a minute, the towel's soaked through with bright red blood.

"Squeeze harder." My heart speeds up at the sight of all that blood. "You need to use a lot of pressure to stop the bleeding."

"Will someone please answer the fucking phone?" Eddie shuffles into the kitchen, eyes half-closed against what is clearly a massive hangover. The phone stops ringing, and in the quiet, my brother finally notices the blood-soaked paper towel. "Holy crap, Mom," he says. "Who'd ya kill?"

The phone starts ringing again and my mother glares at it.

"I'll get it," I say, heading over.

"No!" My mom grabs my arm with her good hand and for the second time that day, nails dig into my skin. "Ignore the phone," she says harshly as I yelp in pain. Without the pressure on the cut, blood starts to run down her arm, dripping off her elbow, landing with moist plops on the stone tile.

"You're going to need stitches," my brother says, looking a little queasy. "It's bleeding too hard." The blood flows like a leaky faucet, *plink, plink, plink,* and we all stand there for a moment, frozen at the sight, before my mom curses under her breath. I hand her a new towel while she calls on the intercom for my dad to come from his workshop in the garage.

He hurries in, wiping greasy hands on a shop towel. Short and built like a brick, wide and solid, he isn't much taller than me, but is very strong. "Built like a tank," he likes to boast. He's always been good with his hands, and even after he retired, he couldn't bring himself to stop tinkering. His hair is dark and matted with sweat, his face florid and red. The workshop is part of the oversized, unair-conditioned garage, and even with a small window unit, it gets scorching hot. Still, it's his favorite place in the house. As he enters the kitchen, his eyes are immediately drawn to the blood-soaked towel my mom is clutching. A soft expletive of surprise escapes him. His eyes flick from one of us to the next to make sure this is the only emergency.

"What did the other guy look like?" he says.

It's enough to bring a wan smile to my mom's lips.

"My knife slipped," she says apologetically. "And I sharpened them yesterday. Sliced my finger but good."

He eyes the tomatoes as if looking for the tip of her finger among them.

"I'm fine," she says, her voice high.

"Do you need stitches?"

"No, no, I'm fine, it's only a cut." She acts like this isn't a big deal because she's always calm and in control in front of us, but her eyes are too wide and her face is too pale.

"Mom," I say, "it's bleeding really hard. You need to go to a doctor."

"I'm fine. Tell her," she orders my dad.

He looks uneasily between the two of us, then stares at the blood.

"Maybe we should have someone look at this," he says, putting an arm around her. "Just to be safe."

"I don't know why you're all making such a fuss."

My dad puts a gentle hand on her shoulder. It's the most I've seen them interact in a week. "Let's go, Linda. Can't hurt to have them take a look."

My mom's shoulders slump in defeat. As my dad leads her to the door, she looks back.

"You kids eat," she instructs me. "Everything's ready to go."

"Good luck, Mom."

She nods grimly and the two of them head out to the ER, my mom clutching her hand, the cut still bleeding. Wetting another paper towel, I wipe the blood off the floor. The edges of each drop have already started to dry and I need to scrub them off the travertine tiles.

I dump the salad and pick up the offending knife, a six-inch Shun Ken Onion with a curved blade, and carefully place it in the sink to wash later. Its wicked edge glints like a malevolent eye.

Eddie and I sit side by side at the massive island in the suddenly quiet kitchen like two strangers at a bar. The sound of our silverware clanking on our plates doesn't fill the silence.

"Jesus," my brother says, rubbing a hand through his shaggy hair. "That was crazy." Then he belches.

"Gross," I say.

He grins.

Nothing pisses my brother off, nothing hurts his feelings. He's a solid wooden block of a person, close to six feet tall and very broad, my dad's build with height from my mom's side of the family. Lately though, he's been more of a sodden, alcoholic wooden block that is about seventy pounds overweight. He has the same basic coloring that my sister and I have: fair skin, dark hair with reddish glints, and sea-colored eyes. But unlike Natasha's creamy complexion or my tanned one, Eddie's skin is blotchy, and he has red veiny cheeks, puffy eyes and hair in a permanent state of greasy dishevelment.

I study him out of the corner of my eye, wondering if I should tell him what Natasha said about the money.

"Natasha's back," I tell him. "It didn't go well."

"It never does," he says, shrugging. He takes a huge scoop of the broccoli-chicken casserole.

"I'm worried about her—"

"Did I ever tell you about Berlin?" he asks at the same time. "Yes."

He ignores me and continues. "I was there with these five guys and then these crazy hot girls came up to us and said there was this private party and did we want to go?" I tune out the rest. I've heard versions of this story that take place in France, Thailand, Peru and New York. Everywhere my brother went, people seemed to sense that he had money and was happy to spend it. One million dollars bought Eddie two years of being the life of the party, of being the guy everyone wanted to hang out with. When the money was gone, the party ended and all he had left was a bunch of stories that sound remarkably similar, once you take out geography.

The phone rings throughout dinner. Exchanging a glance each time, my brother and I ignore it. Eventually Eddie walks over and disconnects the phone from the wall jack. Then he clicks on the television mounted above the cabinets and we ignore each other too.

* * *

My parents return around midnight, looking old and tired.

"You didn't need to wait for us, sweetheart," my dad says when he sees me curled on the couch. Eddie has retreated to the den to catch up on European soccer scores.

"How did it go?" There's a massive bandage around my mom's hand. Her thumb is swaddled and gauze wraps the rest of her hand.

"Seven stitches," my dad says.

"It's a scandal, what's going on in the ER," my mom says, her voice about half an octave higher than usual. "We waited four hours for someone to see us! And then some twelve-year-old stabs me with an eight-gauge crochet needle. Jesus Christ!" She shudders, unconsciously cradling her injured hand to her chest. "We need to call Bob." Bob Johnson is the Democratic legislator my parents supported four years ago when they still had money to burn. I'm not sure he's still in office.

My dad shushes her and pats her back. "Come on, honey, let's get you to bed." Then he looks over at me. "You too, Leni. Off to bed." He leans over and kisses the top of my head. "You've got school tomorrow, got to be sharp." I look into his sweet, tired green eyes and kiss his cheek.

"Okay, Dad. Love you."

"Love you too, baby." He lays a warm hand on my head and I close my eyes at his touch. I kiss my mom on the cheek. She smells like sweat and disinfectant. She gives me a sad, wobbly smile, her blue eyes red-rimmed and watery. Then the two of them make their way, walking slowly, fatigue in their every step, to their suite at the back of the house. My steps echo in the empty foyer, the high ceilings, the bare walls as I climb the stairs again. The house is too big for four people. We're swallowed up.

I'll fix it.

My promise echoes in my head. I think of Natasha and shiver, wondering what awful thing she did.

Fix it.

I'd love to, I think. *But how?*

Chapter Five

We moved into the new house my parents had built about a year after the money landed with a thud in their bank account. A mix of Italian, Spanish and classic Florida styles, the house is a mishmash of ideas that don't fit together: the orange tile roof that doesn't go with the pink stucco that doesn't work with the dark, heavy front doors or the Moorish tiled fountain that stopped working last year. The new house was my mom's chance to finally give her younger daughter the bedroom of her dreams. My mom's dreams, not mine. I was almost twelve at the time, but still, always, the baby of the family.

The walls in my room are pink and the windows are draped with silk swags in cream-and-pink stripes. There's a crystal chandelier hanging from a powder-blue ceiling painted with puffy white clouds. A four-poster bed all in cream and lace squats against a wall, and the attached bathroom is worthy of a professional actress: huge lightbulb-lined mirrors, a sunken tub and a mosaic of Cinderella stepping into her glass slipper. I hated everything about my room from the first second I saw it. Except for the ceiling, which I couldn't even see while lying in bed because of the stupid canopy. I planned to put up with it for a couple of years and by the time I was fourteen, tell my mom I was too old for pink and fairy tales. Then we'd paint the walls cream, and sell the bed and buy me a nice normal one, preferably constructed from salvaged wood, with a sustainably made organic mattress.

But by the time I was fourteen, there were already cracks in the foundation, literally and figuratively. People think that rich people don't have problems. That fancy appliances don't break, that expensive houses aren't shoddily built. People are wrong. Because the house was built so close to the water, the sand under it shifted. Within three years, the house needed to be shored up and pinned. It also turned out that in his hurry to meet his building deadlines, the contractor had skipped a few steps, like lining the floors with a moisture barrier before laying the hardwood planks, or connecting the plumbing in my bathroom to the main sewer line. The family-room floor warped and buckled within two years and all the water from my tub and the sink drained under the house, a big part of the reason the foundation shifted. By the time my parents realized it was a construction issue, the real estate market had started to turn and the contractor was long gone, having declared bankruptcy and fled the state. On the bright side, I used the bathroom down the hall and Cinderella wasn't an issue anymore.

Eddie was back with us by then, moping because all his money was gone. Natasha had sunk her money into Steeped and Emmett's tattoo parlor in Tennessee and she was working fifteen-hour days to make sure her shop succeeded. It became clear to me that money, even copious amounts like my parents had won, didn't last without thoughtful planning. It seemed selfish and petty to whine about wall colors. Besides, I had my share too, a million dollars sitting pretty in a trust fund, growing slowly in an interest-bearing account. When I was eighteen, I'd have my chance to spend it as I saw fit. Which wouldn't be on travel and parties like my brother, or a tea shop like my sister. I was nearly eleven when my parents won the lottery, which meant I had years to think about the best way to spend a million dollars, and I had plans. Plans that I regretfully put aside when the obvious became clear. Seven years after they won a 70-million-dollar jackpot, taking home 22 after the lump payment and taxes, there was nothing left. Except for my trust fund.

Next week the money becomes accessible, and for all their talk about how I should live it up, it's obvious my parents expect me to hand over the money. My million will keep all of us sheltered, clothed and fed for years to come. There is nothing better that I could spend it on. I keep telling myself that. I feel like a bad person when I don't believe it. The money could pay for all my schooling through my PhD. The Marine Rescue Aquarium could use the money to build better rehabilitation tanks for the animals they rescue. A million could save thousands of wetland acres from developers, and the Everglades always need help. Eddie and Natasha got to spend their money pursuing their dreams and now, because I'm the youngest, I won't get to spend mine the way I choose.

Then I remind myself that I choose to spend it taking care of my parents. I would be the worst daughter in the world if when my parents needed help, I spent the money on something else.

I keep telling myself that. And in a week and a half, there won't be anything to say anymore. I'll hand over the money, apply for college loans and that will be the end of that. Except here was Natasha saying not to. And some terrifying angel getting involved.

It's very late, but I'm unsettled and spooked, so instead of sleeping, I shove my pillow out of the way and Google Michael again. This time, following the random rabbit hole of links and more links, I end up reading a passage from the book of Daniel, something I've never read before.

Three Jewish scholars are brought as captives to serve in the court of Nebuchadnezzar, a powerful king. One day, he builds an idol and commands that when a certain piece of music plays, all must fall down and worship before it. The Jewish scholars refuse; their religion prohibits worshiping idols. Incensed by their disobedience, Nebuchadnezzar threatens to burn them in his fiery furnace.

They don't budge.

"God will deliver us from the burning fiery furnace," they say.

Nebuchadnezzar has his men build the fire to seven times its usual heat. He offers the Jewish scholars one last chance to save themselves but they remain confident that the Lord will protect them. The king watches as his soldiers tie the men and push them in, so that they fall down, bound, into the fire.

But they do not burn.

"Lo," cries Nebuchadnezzar, "I see four men loose, walking in the midst of the fire and they have no hurt."

From inside the roaring inferno the figures walk out. The three Jewish men are not hurt, their clothes are not singed, their hair carries no smell of the fire. At that moment, Nebuchadnezzar understands that these young men are under God's protection.

Most scholars believe the fourth figure was the archangel Michael. It's part of the reason many faiths see him as their special protector. The text doesn't explain where the fourth figure disappeared to after leading the men out of the fire.

"So this is a good thing you're doing?" I ask out loud. But Michael doesn't answer.

Sleep remains elusive.

Padding down the stairs, I creep out to the back of the house, feeling the need for fresh air.

It might be something like a sin to build so close to the water, but the view from the patio is amazing. Huddling on a musty-smelling lounge chair, I hug my knees and watch moonlight catch and sparkle on the water. The house looms behind me like a giant beast, the garish pink stucco walls a dull beige under the flat silver light of a three-quarter moon. Tiny airplanes land over at the Tampa airport; occasional pinprick headlights flash by from cars out late in the Bradenton suburbs across the bay, modern fireflies.

It seems impossible to tell my parents that the money we've been living off, the moment that changed us forever, came from a shady deal Natasha made. That I shouldn't give them the money in my trust fund. They'd have Natasha committed within twenty-four hours. And maybe me with her.

I'd take a trip into the fiery furnace over letting down my family like that.

I could pretend that my attack this afternoon was the work of some troublemaker, my vision merely a hallucination as a result of a concussion. There's a very large part of me that wants to do that. Ignore Natasha's advice, forget her crazy story and laugh off my angel encounter. I would too, except for the way Natasha's words stay and resonate within me. *That money is cursed.* There's definitely some truth in that. Eddie went from a successful, if middle-of-the-road, college student to a borderline-alcoholic, twenty-seven-year-old college dropout. Every once in a while he mentions signing up for classes, returning to school, but soon he's back in his room, watching television, bingeing on fast food and endless bags of chips. Natasha always suffered from a want/got gap, wanting too much and happy too little, but even she, in the aftermath of the win, seems worse off, a whirlwind of planning and travel and work that never ceases, and now she's on the verge of some mental collapse. My parents abandoned the family business they started twenty years ago. My dad was an electrician, my mom the office manager/

secretary and accountant. They always said they loved their jobs, they loved being a team, that they would continue working even if they won the lottery. Until they actually won the lottery. Within two months of the win, they put a recording on voicemail saying the business was temporarily closed.

Idle hands are the devil's playthings. It was one of my bubbie's favorite sayings long before we ever won. It isn't healthy not to work. It's not normal. Maybe that's a big part of the problem. My parents certainly aren't a team. Half the time my dad doesn't even come in from his workshop for dinner.

Then there's me. I shiver thinking about it from the angel's perspective. One foot out the door, eager to get away. Willing to give my parents my trust fund, but not my time. If nothing else, Michael's visit reminds me that there's more I can do for my family than hand over a truckful of cash, though that's probably what they would prefer, given the choice.

It takes me a while to define the stomach-churning brew of emotions swirling inside of me. Fear, obviously. Awe. A pinch of disbelief. A few tablespoons of unworthiness. A healthy splash of resentment and helpless confusion. And underneath it all, under the finishing, lingering flavor of this emotional stew, there is a hint of comfort. Confirmation of divine existence is not something I ever expected to receive. Everybody who believes in God relies on faith, but suddenly I have something more than that to work with.

I have to talk to Natasha about this. I need her to make sense of this mess. Even though it's almost two in the morning, I call her and leave a message. There's no way she's sleeping. I wait, hugging my knees, my cell phone lying passively by my hip. I keep checking my cell's (clear) signal, the (ample) battery life. I text her a couple of times. She must be awake.

Call me. We need to talk.

The mosquitoes find me. I stubbornly refuse to leave my seat. She'll call.

After an hour, I trudge up the grand staircase, exhausted but wired at the same time, the phone still in my hand. I text her again.

I lie in bed and place my cell phone on the pillow next to me, waiting for it to buzz. In the morning, still curled on my side, I wake up facing my phone.

Natasha never called.

Chapter Six

With only eight days left before my birthday, I follow the scribbled directions to room B-14 in Laufer Hall through the labyrinth of Safety Harbor Community College, the massive, popular choice of twenty-seven thousand Floridians. The landscaping runs heavy on Spanish moss–draped live oaks, lending the ten-year-old campus a historic, timeless quality.

High school started a few weeks ago but my high school chemistry teacher last year recommended that I take marine chemistry at the local community college this year and it seemed like a good idea at the time: a nice bright mark on my transcript for college admissions. But I'm not prepared for the hustle and bustle of so many people. Half the buildings don't show numbers, the names on two of them have apparently changed since the online map was scanned, so directions that made perfect sense at home don't make a bit of sense here on campus. I hunch my shoulders and duck my head, like a little box turtle hoping to tuck into her shell and hide until this goes away.

If you're going to be a turtle, I tell myself fiercely, *try to be a snapper.*

The common areas are starting to clear as people head into their classrooms, and I have about three minutes to find my room. People are already seated by the time I find B-14.

It's a small room with a large whiteboard at the front where the professor is standing, and rows of battered, badly aligned, blue plastic bucket seats with tiny attached desks. The door is at the front of the room, to the left of the teacher, and everyone's heads turn my way as the door swings open.

"Hi," I whisper and, with my head down, hurry to the first open seat, which happens to be in the front row. *Crap,* I think, feeling eyes boring into my back. *Nice entrance.*

"Welcome, everyone. I think we're all here now," she says, glancing my way. "We have a lot to cover this semester. Let's begin."

She outlines what we'll study, the major issues of marine chemistry, and I forget about the people behind me, forget about the fact that they're all older, and feel excited about learning something that I want to do for the rest of my life. She's like a missionary preaching salvation to us savages, except she isn't asking us to open our hearts, she's asking us to open our minds.

When she calls for a ten-minute break halfway through

the ninety-minute class, I blink and reluctantly leave my seat. Most of the students congregate in the open-air hallway outside the room. A few smokers light up, while other students hustle over to the vending machines around the corner for a sugar/caffeine hit. We chat, trading names that I instantly forget and basic information about each other. Turns out there are two other students my age, homeschoolers who are taking community-college classes and amassing college credits. One of them is three credits shy of an associate's degree and she's sixteen. There's a girl in a vintage Hello Kitty shirt who recently switched majors for the second time. A couple of guys who thought this would be an easy science class grumble about the professor's lecture but the rest of us ignore them.

There's one student who stays conspicuously quiet, leaning against a metal pillar, apart from the group but close enough to listen. I barely noticed him when I first stepped out, too engaged with the rest of the group, but after a while I feel his eyes drilling into my back. Our break is almost over when it finally sinks in. I do a mental double take as I recognize the slouch.

I know him.

As if he's been biding his time, waiting for me to notice him, as soon as our eyes meet he slowly makes his way over to me. Wearing low-slung jeans and flip-flops, hands shoved in his pockets, he's taller than I remember, his dark hair cut short now, and so ridiculously good-looking it hurts me. For a second, I forget that I've never liked him, that I don't like anything about him. For a second, I forget to lie to myself.

He doesn't say anything to me. Just holds my gaze, wearing an inscrutable expression.

Gavin was that guy my freshman year, the magnetic rock to everyone else's iron ore. I can't count how many girls had crushes on him. How many people laughed at his jokes or found their way to his lunch spot on the quad. We ended up taking a computer-science class together, but I tried to stay out of his way as much as possible. On principle. He was too cocky and arrogant and everyone else thought way too much of him and his pranks and his sharp wit. When he ended up getting arrested for hacking, we were all shocked, of course. But Gavin has a way of turning lemons into advantages, and despite the stint in juvie, the last I heard he managed to score a full ride to Tech. I can't imagine what he's doing here at SHCC.

As I look at him now, a hot blush rises for no good reason.

"Hi," I say into the awkward silence. "I think we went to high school together a couple of years ago? I'm Leni."

"Yeah," he says. "I know."

Then why are you staring at me like a psycho?

"Gavin, right?"

He nods curtly.

"Welcome back," I say, vaguely referencing the ginormous elephant in the room.

He nods again and stalks past me into class.

Okaaaay. I guess he prefers that we all ignore the giant elephant. I'll try to remember that for next time we don't have a conversation.

Once class resumes, I have a hard time keeping up with the

teacher. Gavin sits at the end of the row about halfway back with an open laptop obscuring his lower face.

It would be a lie to say I haven't thought about him since he left school. People still talk about some of his more legendary pranks—no one has been able to match the statue of our school rival's mascot, the Sand Crab, on a cafeteria tray in our school's trophy case—but seeing him now, after two years, I realize that it wasn't a mistake that half the school idolized him. There *is* something charismatic about him.

I promptly renew my vow to stay away from him, shared class notwithstanding.

Throughout my musings and the professor's lecture, Gavin has been steadily typing. The professor glances at the seating chart and calls out, "Gavin Armand." The typing stops. "What are some of the benefits of a chemical approach to ocean science?"

I'm the only one who isn't surprised when he answers clearly and intelligently.

"The advantages are that measurements are reproducible and a small sample is representative of the whole." He has a deep, even voice. Calm and thoughtful. At complete odds with his jerky-slacker attitude. "Chemical compounds are also markers of the past, meaning they can uncover biological or geological events while giving scientists a good look at current marine dynamics."

The professor blinks and then smiles like a woman who has found a Godiva chocolate in her bag of M&M's. A couple of students share glances and roll their eyes, but I'm with the professor. Gavin's brilliant. That's a big part of the problem. Always was.

At the end of class, she sets up a sign-up sheet.

"You'll each need a lab partner," she says. "There will be three labs during this course and I reserved the lab for our class to use on Friday mornings. You'll be graded on the lab reports that you turn in. This is an advanced-level class and I expect excellence from you all."

She looks at us, making eye contact.

"Lab can provide you with hands-on learning that nothing in the classroom can provide. Lab is where it's at, people. So make a commitment to it and see it through." She gazes at us sternly; then apparently feeling she's made her point, she nods. "Okay, you can go."

All the students gather their things and shuffle out, pausing by the sheet to sign up for a lab time and partner. I hustle over to the professor to discuss getting a note to give to my high school. I didn't factor in for lab time and I'll need a valid excuse for missing three Friday mornings of world-history class. By the time she scrawls a note and signs it, everyone has signed up and left. There's only one name without a partner. It figures. With a heavy heart and sinking feeling of gloom, I sign up to be Gavin's lab partner. Our first lab is tomorrow. It's only three times, I tell myself. Keep your head down, don't try to be friends and you'll get through it.

My heart speeds up as I approach the familiar storefront, the royal-blue-and-cream awning shading the front door with a cup of tea etched on the glass and Steeped written in dainty letters under it. I've been trying all day to think of what to say to my sister.

"Natasha?" The fruity smell of tea greets me as I step into the cool, dark shop. An iced raspberry-mint tea would be awesome right now.

"Tasha?" I call out again, heading straight to the back. "Do you need a break? I can stay until dinner." *Maybe she's feeling better today.* Maybe we'll figure something out together. Maybe it isn't as bad as I fear and she's being hard on herself.

There aren't any customers at the shop and even the stereo is silent. It's almost eerie.

"Hello?" My heart beats faster. Again, absurd, out-of-proportion worry for Natasha suddenly takes over. I rush toward the back of the shop.

"Hey, if it isn't Little Sister." Stepping out of the back room, John Parker walks up to the counter, smiling a broad greeting. I stop abruptly, my satchel bumping into me, before continuing slowly. It's beyond weird for John to be at the shop so soon after Natasha's trip. I've never really liked John and that was before he asked me out on a date a couple of months ago. This with him being at least ten years my senior. Then all those smiles and pats on the back that lingered too long made sense.

I didn't tell Natasha that he asked me out, since she'd probably fire him. As clichéd as it sounds, good help really is hard to find, and John has stuck with her for a year and a half, longer than anyone else. He's a good enough assistant manager, and none of the customers have ever complained. But I hate being alone with him. There's something creepy about his too-large hands; his big, even teeth; and the hair that seems snapped on, like a plastic piece on a LEGO figurine.

"Where's Natasha?"

"Your sister needed a spa day," he says, smirking, like, *oh, you silly girls.* "And I was glad to help out."

"That's big of you," I say. "Why is the music off?"

He looks up at the speakers, as if to ask them why. "You have such wonderful attention to detail." He beams, as if he's paid me a tremendous compliment.

I wait. He leans forward, elbows resting on the counter, smiling in anticipation, as if we're exchanging witty retorts and the ball's in my court.

"How long did Natasha say she'd be gone?"

His smile dims a bit. But gamely he continues lobbing his creepy version of charm my way. "Oh, I don't know. Until the evening, at least." This said in hearty tones of *Good news!*

"Tell her to call me, okay?" I head for the door.

"You're welcome to stay here."

"Oh, thanks," I say, with exaggerated gratitude. *It's my sister's shop, asshole.* "But I have a ton of homework. I'd hate to get detention." I love reminding him how young I am. "Then I'd get grounded." His smile dims further. "Lose TV privileges."

I should stop before he realizes I'm mocking him.

"Don't forget, tell Natasha to call me. It's important." Then before he can say anything else, I quickly leave the shop.

Sweating in the humid heat, I'm uneasy as I mess with my bike lock. John's presence at the store doesn't make sense.

Natasha would never miss a day of work after a long trip. She's ignoring me, maybe avoiding me, and that doesn't make sense either. There's something about John that's grosser than usual, which is saying a lot. In his own way, he's as screwed up as Natasha.

Chapter Seven

My mom sits at the breakfast bar, perched on a stool with her back to me. I'm in no mood to recount how class went, and strangely reluctant to mention that Gavin is back in town. Seeing him again after all these years has stirred up some weird feelings. Like how hard I tried not to like him and how awkward it's going to be having him as my lab partner. Glancing over my shoulder to make sure Mom didn't notice me walk by, I have a clear shot to the staircase, but something about the way she's sitting stops me.

Her face is buried in her hands. There's a mess of paperwork on the counter. Even from the doorway I can see they're all bank statements and bills. The phone is next to her.

"Mom?" Her shoulders stiffen at the sound of my voice but

she doesn't turn around. "You okay?" But damn it, it's obvious she's not. "Bad news, Mom?"

She wipes her eyes roughly, shaking her head before turning to face me. Her hair is messy and her blue eyes are red-rimmed and puffy.

"No, no, sweetie. Everything's fine. I'm surprised you're not still at Steeped." She touches her hair, smoothing it in place, a nervous habit of hers. Her bandaged thumb catches in her hair and she hisses in painful surprise. Then she grabs the paperwork, shoving it in a haphazard pile, covering it like it's a stack of porn.

I reach out to touch her good hand and she jumps with a guilty conscience.

"You don't have to pretend, Mom."

The phone rings and the sudden noise makes her eyes well with tears. It rings and rings and we both wait silently for the shrill intruder to stop.

It stops after five rings.

"Mom," I say. "I can handle it. What's going on?"

There's a mulish look on her face. My mother has never admitted we're having financial difficulties. She likes everyone to think everything is perfect. And certainly, in front of me, the baby, she likes to be fully in charge, a soccer mom in her domain. But I'm not ten and it's my trust fund that she's counting on. If there were any other way, she wouldn't let me spend a penny of it on her. Which makes it that much harder not to give it all to her. She deserves it. She deserves everything good I have to give her.

"Okay, then, I'll guess," I say, sitting on the stool next to her. "The bank wants to foreclose on the house because we can't pay the mortgage?"

Her chin wobbles.

"It's okay, Mom." I lay my hand over hers, the one that covers the paperwork pile. The bandaged one. "I've known for a while there are problems."

"It's not a problem," she says stubbornly. "There have been some misunderstandings." She glares at the phone. "There have been . . . miscommunications. That's the problem with a big corporation, there's not a human being to talk to. Every time I call, someone else answers the phone and no one knows what the other person promised, or what agreements we made. One person agrees to something and then the next time I call, some idiot says there's no record of what we agreed on. It's so aggravating!" Then she catches herself, and tries to smile at me. It's an unnatural smile and I feel pained about how oblivious I've been to her distress. Some of what I'm thinking must show on my face, and unlike me, my mom doesn't miss it. She waves her free hand as if blowing away a bad smell. "None of it really matters. We'll sort it all through. By next week, I'm sure we'll see eye to eye." She sneaks a quick glance at me to gauge my reaction.

I squirm with guilt that I'm not being honest with her, that I'm letting her assume all these financial problems will disappear next week. Because maybe they won't. More and more I think that "fixing it" is not fixing my parents' debts.

"Really," I say noncommittally.

She nods a bit uncertainly. I won't look at her, suddenly

furious. *It's your own fault,* I think. *You created this mess. You and Dad blew away more money than the GDP of some countries.* Some of what I'm thinking must show on my face again. My mom presses her lips together, then forces her hand off the paperwork and makes a show of examining a small chip in her manicure. It's fuchsia, very Florida lady-of-the-manor. She used to wear only clear nail polish, back before the win. I remember her saying it was both flattering and practical since you can never tell when it chips.

"And of course this is coming at the absolutely worst time," she says, in the false cheerful voice of the put-upon. "I'm still waiting to hear from the florist if the lilies came in like she promised they would. The caterer called to say they won't be able to serve chilled berries in cream, your very favorite dish, because there was flooding in California that ruined their raspberry crop. Honestly! I told them they grow berries in Chile, what's the big deal? Drive down to Costco and pick up some. But they insist no one is selling them. So now we have to figure out what to serve instead. What do you think of smoothies served in tiny shot glasses? That could be cute, right? Maybe with a little swirl of whipped cream on top? I saw some in a magazine and they were adorable."

I keep forgetting she's planning a big party for my eighteenth birthday.

"I thought we were getting the food from Natasha's vendors," I say in disbelief.

"We're getting the scones and finger sandwiches but I

thought we needed a couple of signature dishes to jazz it up. A tea party is a nice idea, but we don't want to look cheap."

"Mom, I don't even want a party," I say, for the millionth time. "I don't need one."

Florists? Caterers? The only reason I agreed to a party was because it would be at Steeped and, I assumed, practically free. It's not like I have a ton of friends to invite anyway.

"Who's coming?" I ask in sudden horror.

"Not that many people, really. Although a lot of people haven't RSVP'd, which means, of course, that they might be coming anyway."

"How many, though?"

"Fifty?" she guesses.

I close my eyes. *Come on.* I want to shake her. *We're broke!*

"You were born three weeks early," my mom says suddenly. "It caught us completely by surprise. I couldn't even believe I was having true labor. I kept thinking it was some cramps, nothing serious, until it got so intense that Dad called the neighbors, told them to come watch the kids and pushed me in the car."

I've heard this story before. I used to ask her to tell it to me all the time.

"Thirty minutes after we arrived at the hospital, you were born. I barely made it to the room in the maternity ward and the whole time, as I'm trying to breathe through the labor pains, I say, 'It can't be the baby, it isn't time yet!'" She laughs at the memory and looks at me with her eyes shining. "And there you were, tiny and perfect. The nurse wrapped you up and handed you to me. You had been screaming but as soon as you felt me, you stopped crying and looked up at me with your big, beautiful green eyes and I said, 'Hi there,' and Dad said, 'Well, what do you know, it is the baby.' We all laughed and laughed because there you were. You were so beautiful that all the nurses on the floor stopped by to take a look. My little miracle." She swallows. "I never understood why you were born early. But now I do. Everything happens for a reason." She draws a shaky breath. "We can't wait three weeks, honey. The bank wants to start foreclosure procedures next week. Your birthday is coming right in the nick of time."

I suddenly unwish wanting her to flat-out ask for the money. It's so much worse this way.

"I don't know what we'd do otherwise." She wipes her eyes, leaving smears of black liner on her fingers.

"Mom . . . ," I start.

"I didn't want to tell you," she says. "None of this should concern you. I hate that you know any of it."

"But—"

"I know, you're old enough to handle it," she finishes for me, misunderstanding what I was trying to say. "I know you are, sweetie." She touches my face softly and squeezes my shoulder. "You're so grown-up and amazing. You are. You are an incredible person but to me you'll always be my little girl. My perfect little baby surprise. And this financial mess isn't anything you should have to deal with."

"But, Mom," I say. "What's wrong with our old house? I liked it. I liked our neighbors. I liked the kids who lived on the corner. I liked our orange tree."

She smiles fondly.

"It was a sweet little house. We had a lot of happy years there."

"Exactly."

But she doesn't get it.

"Once we get this mess fixed, I'll have a big party," she says, with that old spark of excitement. "We'll spruce up the house a bit, you know, get some new furniture, freshen up the paint, and then I'll invite the old block. What do you think? Something to look forward to, isn't it?"

"No, Mom! No more parties!" I want to bang my head against the wall. "We don't need new furniture! We don't need a big party! I don't need a birthday party! We don't have the money and I don't have fifty friends! This party isn't even for me."

"I'm sorry," she says, clearly offended. "I thought you'd appreciate a party for your birthday. I've put a lot of time and work into it. And believe me, I kept the cost down. It would have been much more expensive if I hadn't pinched every penny until it squeaked!"

"We should move back to our old neighborhood," I blurt out. "We never sold our old house, we could move back into it. We lived there just fine and we could do it again and everything will go back to the way it was."

She forces a titter and rolls her eyes.

"Move back there? Honey, you don't remember, but it's not a great neighborhood. There were break-ins. The school zone is awful. There was a drug bust three houses down a couple of years ago. There's no way we'd live there. Not to mention that your memory is playing tricks on you. If you saw our tiny little 3/2 now, you'd never be able to live there. Old terrazzo floors, a tiny, sandy yard full of fire ants and weeds."

"This isn't about me, Mom," I snap back. "You're the one who's too good to live there now."

She's out of her seat, rising to her full height.

"How dare you talk to me like that, young lady." The fond, proud look is gone. "You are not too old to be grounded! When did you become such a spoiled, ungrateful child?"

I stand up too, and we're the same height. Our fists are clenched by our sides and both of us have our chins forward in a pugnacious tilt.

"I am going to say it, because you need to hear it. How did we get here? You and Dad got us here!" I gesture at the bills but in my anger, I misjudge and knock the pile over. They scatter and flutter like birds set free. We both stare at the mess. Bills and statements are everywhere, on the floor, on the counter, on the chairs.

"Oh, crap," I say sadly.

"It wasn't our fault, honey," my mom says, her anger deflated in the face of this mess, physical and metaphorical. "We had the worst luck. The investments . . . then the economy turned at the worst moment, no one could have known that would happen. . . ."

I don't want to hear the excuses. With a sigh, I kneel down to pick up the papers.

"No," she says, stopping me. "I'll do it."

"But it's my fault. Let me help."

"No," she says firmly. "I'll clean up. Go do your homework. You don't want to fall behind."

She's not furious anymore and neither am I. But nothing has been cleared up and I still haven't told her I might not give over the money. It's hard to do it in the face of her quiet dignity and defeat.

"We can't move back to the old house," she says tiredly, kneeling by the bills on the floor. "We haven't paid the taxes on it in three years. There's almost ten thousand dollars due. The county's putting it up for auction soon." She speaks so quietly, it's almost a whisper.

My deflating anger leaves me empty and all stretched out. I bend down again to help pick up the mess but she shoos me away. "Go do your homework."

"Okay, Mom." I kiss her cheek. "I love you, you know."

She nods, still kneeling, and I can't see her face.

"I know you do," she says, her voice nearly muffled. "I know."

I leave her on her knees in the kitchen, picking up the mess we all made.

Climbing the wide staircase, grasping the railing, its tendrils of wrought iron like frozen vines from some enchanted land, I have never felt more alone.

Give all my trust away? I ask, my heart pounding at the thought of an angel visit right here in my house. Yet I have to ask. *How will that fix this?*

But angels don't answer unsolicited questions. Maybe he's busy with other chores. All is quiet as I slowly trek upstairs.

There are only us lost human souls in the house and we have to make our way as best we can.

I used to be dismissive of people who prayed to God for answers. My literal, scientific mind used to believe that unless some heavenly voice answered you with the correct answer, you were wasting your time. You might as well be asking your invisible friend what she thinks about the situation.

Yet even without a dramatic reply, simply asking the question calms me. Giving the money away is the starting point. But it has to be done right, or it's as pointless as all the spending my family has already done. My money has to buy the right thing.

I have eight days to figure out what that is.

Jennifer was the first one who noticed Aiden wasn't acting right. Drew ignored her at first. All kids go through weird phases. Jennifer overreacted a lot, every fever meant a trip to the doctor, every scrape was gooped in antibacterial gel. Aiden was fine. Of course he was fine. He ate nothing but organic food. Slept in organic-cotton pajamas and played with wooden toys made in America and certified lead free. How could anything be seriously wrong with a three-year-old? But as Aiden started losing what the pediatrician called "milestones," even Drew started to worry.

You never want to hear the word "cancer." It's a nightmare, a death sentence, your body's betrayal of you. But to hear it said about your kid? Your sweet, funny little guy? That was a knife thrust straight in your gut, then twisted.

"But I did everything right," Jennifer wailed when the pediatric oncologist delivered the news. Tears ran unchecked down her face. "I did everything I was supposed to."

Drew, who hadn't cried since he was ten and fumbled the pop fly that cost his team the game, felt his eyes prickle as tears overflowed. My boy, he kept thinking. My boy.

It was the start of hell. They didn't even realize, they didn't have a clue what lay in store for them. The modern-day equivalent of a hall of torture that you were supposed to submit your toddler to willingly, that you were supposed to be grateful for. And they were, of course. They were pathetically grateful to all the nurses, the teams of doctors, the therapists, dietitians and psychiatrists, everyone who was so willing to give everything they had to try and fix what was wrong with Aiden. Aiden, who cried when he saw anyone wearing scrubs. Who knew the way to the hospital better than the way to the park. Who had had more surgeries by the time he was six than most people have in a lifetime.

Then, on top of the agony of watching their son fight so bravely for his life, on top of the cruel waiting game to see if the cancer would come back, and dealing with it when it did, again and again, there were the bills. More than they could handle. More than anyone could. They always thought they had decent health coverage, until they realized they didn't. You'd have to be a millionaire to handle your share of the bills.

Which was when someone mentioned that one of their former neighbors had won the lottery a couple of years back. One of those Powerball jackpots. If God cared about us at all, Drew thought bitterly, we'd win so we could pay these bills. Then again, if God cared about them at all, pediatric oncology wouldn't be a field of medicine.

Before the diagnosis, Drew couldn't imagine ever asking anyone for a loan, let alone some stranger. Before the diagnosis, they paid cash for their house, cash for their cars; they didn't believe in mortgages and car loans. Before Aiden got sick, there were a lot of things Drew couldn't imagine. He still didn't want to do it, but Jennifer had no such qualms.

"If Aiden can get stuck with a needle six times while that Cro-Magnon nurse Heidi searches for a vein," she said, spewing rage at him as if he were the one responsible, "you can certainly tuck your pride and see if someone will help us." They were fighting a lot by then. About money. About Aiden. About everything. They were close to losing the house. They had taken out a huge mortgage to pay the hospital, and now those monthly payments jostled with the never-ending doctors' bills for the best and juiciest parts of Drew's paycheck. They probably had a couple more months before the bank called in their mortgage. They'd already traded in their cars like a car commercial played in reverse, driving away with a clunker and leaving their excellent sedan behind.

So for Aiden, for all of them, he went to meet the guy, the millionaire, who actually seemed like a decent sort. Drew swore up and down that he'd pay it back. Every bit. Every penny. And he meant it, though how he ever would was a problem that seemed small compared with everything else he was facing.

When the guy wrote him the check, as easy as pie, Drew felt

tears prickle behind his eyes. Tears of gratitude. Of envy at how easy some people had it.

"It'll make a huge difference," Drew said, clutching the check to his chest like a talisman. "This will make all the difference." But at the same time he knew it wasn't enough. It would never be enough.

Chapter Eight

So where did all the money go?

The dolphin, of course. A share in a helicopter that we used twice. A custom RV that my parents sold after three years for a fraction of what they bought it for. A boat that Eddie trashed with some college buddies. Another one that slowly rusted in the marina. This stupid house and all its troubles. I did my share too. I begged for an iPad on the day they came out. Took an amazing cruise with my parents to the Galápagos for my thirteenth birthday (I dropped hints for a month to avoid a repeat of the twelfth-birthday disaster). The RV was my idea, too; I had visions of touring all the national parks during one epic summer road trip. The most we ever did, though, was drive it to Disney and "camp" for a week.

There were investments too. A failed sushi bar in Ocala. Condominiums in Tampa. A resort, or mall, or something like that, in Costa Rica (that one I tried to talk them out of). A lot of the money disappeared in foolish attempts to make more from investments that were a sure thing.

Then there were all those second cousins once removed. Old high school buddies, looking to reconnect after all these years. And . . . well, they could use a helping hand. They all needed help. Some of them were jerks, looking for a handout, but some of them really did need help. One of them had a very sick child and horrid insurance that wouldn't pay for a vital operation. One of them was struggling to make it through college, loaded down with two jobs and insane loans, and she wasn't sure she'd be able to graduate. One of them had lost his job, had three young kids, and the bank was threatening foreclosure. And couldn't my parents help?

Hardly anyone paid them back. At a rough guess, my parents "lent" a couple of million. All those heartfelt promises to repay were usually empty promises in the end. After the first few times, my parents understood that when they wrote someone a check, they called it a loan when actually it was a gift.

It pisses me off that my folks wasted so much money on the stupid house, the flower arrangements, the trips and clothes and parties, a freaking mall in the rain forest, and I feel sick about my part in the whole fiasco. But when I think of all the people my parents helped, really and truly saved, even if the people themselves no longer felt a debt of gratitude, then I know my parents were on the right track.

So I start with charities. There are people out there who de-serve what we landed a lot more than us. Find a few of them and I'm good to go. I type in a few keywords, and worthy candidates fill my screen. There are programs for wounded veterans. Fos-ter kids. Urban gardens. Sending children to science summer camp. Protecting sea grass in the bay. Restoring oyster beds in the Chesapeake. Providing clean water in the developing world. Promoting literacy. Preventing child abuse. If nothing else, it cheers me up to see that so many people are trying to make the world a better place. But after an hour of surfing websites and testimonials, I've found nothing that really feels right. Nothing sends a shiver of recognition down my spine. This is going to take more than picking a worthwhile charity and dumping my trust fund in their account. It's too easy. It'll need to mean a whole heck of a lot before I turn my back on my family. It needs to be personal.

It's past midnight when I shut off my computer, but sleep eludes me. For the second night in a row, I check the clock at five-minute intervals, unable to turn my brain off. I keep replay-ing the look on my mom's face. How in God's name am I sup-posed to tell her she can't have the money?

I slip out of bed and head to the patio at the back of the house.

Once again, I huddle on one of the faded, musty lounge chairs, staring blindly at the dark water. It doesn't take long before I catch the flickering blue light of late-night television in my peripheral vision. Eddie, up late, in a waking coma in front of the TV. Out of curiosity, I turn to my parents' window and sure enough, there's light glowing around the margins of their heavy lined curtains.

Two in the morning and every one of us is awake in our Florida mansion.

Invasive air potato vines and cat claw vine, with its wicked thorns, have officially taken over our yard in the year since my parents stopped the yard service. They wind through every shrub, pulling down saplings. Spanish needles and prickly crab-grass grow freely in the beds, blurring any lines the landscaper originally intended. Add to that the fact that each of us is fighting some private demon, unable to sleep, and it sounds almost familiar. A story told long ago, some fairy tale about an evil curse and a kingdom under a spell.

The stories always start with a curse. Ours was winning the lottery.

It doesn't matter that it's two in the morning. I have to talk to Natasha.

Natasha has her own place, a condo in a fancy high-rise on the water near Steeped. It's a ten-minute bike ride, and at two a.m. on a Friday, there's no one to do a double take at a girl in pajamas and flip-flops furiously pedaling.

I key in her security code to enter the building and let myself into her condo with the spare key she keeps at our house.

Her apartment is dark, naturally. Hoping I don't scare the living daylights out of her, I carefully open the door to her bedroom.

The plan is to gently shake her awake and let her know I'm not budging until she tells me the full story. But Natasha is

already awake. She sits on her bed, hugging her knees, the identical pose I was in a few minutes ago on the patio. She looks up when the door swings open like she's been waiting for someone to come, like she's barely holding on.

"I'm scared, Leni," she says in a small, high voice. Goose bumps spread across my skin.

"Why?"

"I've done something awful." Her chin quivers. "Something really, really awful. And I'm scared that I can never be forgiven." She begins weeping in hopeless sobs and I freeze at the sight of my confident, sensual older sister reduced to this mess. Not that my last encounter with her was exactly normal, but this verges on a true crisis, a dial-911, hand-this-over-to-the-professionals sort of situation. I could call Mom, but instinctively I know she'd be helpless here. I could dial 911, but the imaginary conversation where I tell the operator that my emergency is my older sister weeping in bed because she had someone rig the lottery doesn't play well in my head. When I catch a whiff of ripe body odor, at least I know where to start.

"Come on." I tug on Natasha's arm, almost encircling her upper arm with my fingers. "There's no point crying in bed. You need a shower. You smell."

Pulling and prodding, I get her out of bed and into the shower. Hers is all sleek and modern, with cold glass tile and chrome fixtures. Her clothes stink of sweat and cigarette smoke. Once she's undressed, the vertebrae in her spine stick out like LEGOs and her ribs are starkly exposed; hip bones jut out. Her

hands are chapped and red, her fingernails raw and bleeding where she's bitten them to the quick.

"In!" I command, ignoring the sad state of her body, and point to the steaming shower. She enters slowly, flinching as the water hits. I scrub her hair, my shirt getting soaked. I hand her a bar of soap to wash her body, and then wait for her to step into the towel I hold outstretched for her.

Once she's clean and wrapped in the towel, I change my sopping shirt for one of hers and grab a pair of fresh, cozy pajamas for Natasha. She still huddles under the towel and I end up dressing her, buttoning the shirt while her hands hang limply at her sides.

She's calmer now; maybe cleanliness really is next to godliness. But when I lead her back to her room and urge her to go to bed, to sleep, she refuses.

"I don't want to sleep," she says. "I have nightmares."

"Natasha." Here's what I want to say: *You're being ridiculous. You're twenty-four. You can't be scared of the dark.* But the words die before I can say them. She looks utterly drained and pathetic.

We stand at an impasse by her bed.

"I'll stay for the night," I finally say. "It's late, anyway."

She sighs, her shoulders slumping, and nods in agreement. We both crawl under the thin cotton blanket and there's a weird adjustment to the fact that there's another person in the bed with me.

Natasha curls on her side away from me. She always runs the AC at full blast and the dark room is freezing. But for once,

I'm glad for the bracing chill. It's very late, but we're not sleeping until she tells me the rest of the story.

"Tasha," I say. "What's really going on?"

She's quiet for a moment and I think she's going to say that she's tired, that she'll tell me in the morning.

"You have to tell me," I insist. "Tell me about this lottery guy. Who is he, what's he like?"

She waits another second, postponing the inevitable.

"He wasn't tall," she finally says. "But there was something about him that made him seem like he was. You know how some people are like that? Like they're bigger than their bodies. I liked that about him. That confidence. Like he always got what he wanted. I loved that about him."

Her voice is soft in the dark, coming from the other side of the bed, eerie and mesmerizing. This is how the whole mess got started. My heart starts beating a little faster.

"Where did you meet him?"

"I was sneaking a smoke in the parking lot at school. And there he was, leaning against one of the cars, smiling like he was in on the joke, you know? Like it was all one big joke. Maybe it was, for him." Natasha laughs in a mirthless sort of huff. "He wore tight jeans, cowboy boots and this amazing calf-skin jacket, all soft and buttery. I really wanted to touch it. He should have looked ridiculous but he made it work. All I could do was look at him and think how sexy he was. His hair was the way I like it, loose, soft, kind of messy." Even after everything that has happened, Natasha's still excited, some part of her is still turned on. There's this tone in her voice that says she doesn't get it, even after all our family has been through. I think about my mom, falling apart in the kitchen, and all I feel is rage.

"Did you know who he was?" What I really want to ask is: *How could you be so stupid, how could you be so blind?*

"At first, no, of course not. No. No. I didn't know, didn't have a clue who he was. I thought he was some really awesome substitute teacher. Undercover narc, maybe. But nothing worse than that."

"And later? When did you find out?" I demand. "Why did you think it would work out well?" I want to shake her poor, withered body until the bones knock together. This thing that she leveled the family with. This false gift. And all of us, shadows awake at night, riddled with guilt we can't understand.

"Leni, it wasn't like that," she says, her voice rising. "It wasn't like that at all. He was so nice, so helpful. And we won! We won seventy million dollars. How was I supposed to know each one of those dollars was a curse? How could I have known that then? I was only seventeen."

We're both breathing heavily and my heart knocks in my chest at the sudden adrenaline rush, but there's nothing to fight and nowhere to hide.

"There *was* something a little scary about him," she finally admits. "I couldn't put my finger on it, but the first thing I did when I saw him was take a step back." I sit up to see her face better, but she stays on her side, her back to me, a pale mound under the washed-out covers. "I keep thinking about that," she says to the wall. "That small step away from him." Her voice is suddenly thick with tears. "He frowned when he saw it. Then he smiled this crooked little smile and started talking. I keep thinking about how some part of me knew I should leave, but I ignored it."

I slide back under the covers, suddenly cold. In the dark we lie back to back, two parentheses facing the wrong direction.

"Natasha . . ." My anger is gone and only a weary sadness is left in its wake.

"All I could think about was that Emmett was leaving. He was enlisting in the army and he was leaving St. Pete and he wasn't coming back. I couldn't stand it. I couldn't let him leave me like that. I was completely obsessed."

I don't remember that time very well—I was only ten. But I remember how worried my parents were about her. How they felt she was crossing some line, passing from youthful intensity into something not-normal, into crazy. Maybe that's what caught his attention in the first place. Maybe she secreted some pheromone, something that said she'd cross any lines, pay any price, and it's what attracted him to her. To take her up on what she was so clearly eager to give away.

"The first few times I saw him, he never asked anything about me," she says, settling into the story. "When he saw me light up the first time, he offered to share some of his smokes. He said they were smoother than anything I'd ever had. What a pickup line, right?"

"A lame one."

She falls silent and I kick myself for interrupting her flow.

"I took one," she says after a pause. "He flicked a gold lighter and as soon as I tasted it, I knew he was telling the truth, it was amazing. He finished before me and he crushed the butt under his heel and said, 'See you later.' And that was it. I watched him walk away as I kept smoking; he never looked back. A couple of days later I saw him outside a coffee shop where I was with some friends. But he only waved and kept going. He was wearing that wonderful leather jacket and looking like he could be a movie star. All my friends were dying to know who he was, asking me how I knew him. So I said we met at a concert, that he was a musician. When I saw him again the next week, I had some crazy thought of going out with him, making Emmett jealous." She laughs hollowly. "God, can you believe that? Seventeen-year-olds are pathetic, aren't they?"

"I guess it depends on the seventeen-year-old."

"Sorry, Leni, I forget how young you are sometimes. You're definitely smarter than I was at your age." That's supposed to make me feel better, but it's not much of a compliment.

"So what happened next? After you tried to date the evil hacker?"

She winces at the bite in my tone.

"I asked him where he got his cigarettes because I wanted to buy some. He reached in his pocket and took out a nearly full pack and handed it to me. He told me they were blended especially for him, and I could keep the pack, he'd get more later. It didn't have a name on it, just a red carton with a gold flame embossed in the center. They had to be really expensive. When I shared them with my friends, everyone went crazy over them. They made us feel so good, mellow but focused, you know?"

I don't nod, I don't move, we're getting to the heart of the story.

"I saw him again a week later by the Vinoy about to cross the street. I ran after him before he could turn the corner. He laughed when he saw me coming, like I made his day. I told him I wanted to buy him a Coke or something. I felt like I owed him for the cigarettes. We ended up hanging out on the veranda at the Vinoy, sitting in rocking chairs and talking. We were there for hours. Leni, it sounds so crazy now, but he totally got me. When he told me a little about himself, I could see that he was like me. Like, how if you really want something, you don't give up. When you love someone, it's with all your heart and soul, you don't leave anything on the table. And the next thing I knew, I was nodding along because finally somebody *got* me. Totally and completely understood how I was put together. Everyone else thought I was crazy to keep chasing after Emmett. No one understood except him."

She sighs deeply.

"I can see how every time we met was a setup. Everything I told him, he already knew. He was telling me the things I wanted to hear. Everything he gave me came with strings attached. By the time he finally revealed that he was more than what he seemed, I'd already known him for a couple of months, I already liked him. I—I trusted him.

"He knew every evil thought I'd ever had, every wish I ever made. He knew it all and he made it sound normal, he made me feel normal. And he promised he could help." She's silent for a moment, remembering it all. "It made sense, everything he said. Someone had to win the lotto, why not us? And I'd be helping the whole family, really. We'd all be millionaires and Mom and Dad wouldn't have to work so hard. I'd have all this money and Emmett would stay with me forever because he wouldn't need a job, he wouldn't need to enlist, I'd take care of him. All he asked in return was that I promise to help him one day if he needed my help. That's all. He didn't ask for my soul. He laughed when I asked him. Just a favor in return for a favor. I kept thinking of that old story of the mouse and the lion."

A prickling of unease flitters across my skin.

"Your soul?" My voice has gone tight and high. "Why would you even ask him that?"

But here's the thing. I know.

"Because he's the devil, Leni. And that's what everyone always says the devil wants."

For a moment, the magnitude of what she's said hangs in the air.

"Natasha," I say, pity and horror and disgust in my voice. "Oh, Natasha."

"He ruined us," Natasha whispered. "He ruined all of us. And then he had me ruin another family."

I'm suddenly furious. This is why Michael came to me. It's because of her. I feel tainted, guilty, even though I've done nothing wrong. "They win the lottery too?" I ask sarcastically.

"No." She stays silent so long I think she isn't going to answer. But after what seems like hours, Natasha speaks again and says the thing I've been waiting to hear, the thing I dread and know is coming.

"I thought when the time came the favor wouldn't be so bad. Years passed and he stayed away and didn't ask for anything. I thought maybe he forgot about me. I thought that if he did come back one day and said he wanted me to do something really bad, I would refuse. I would take whatever punishment he handed out and suffer and not hurt anyone."

Her chin starts quivering and her voice cracks as she keeps talking. "I thought I was strong enough. I thought I was a good person. But he cut off all my options. I couldn't say no."

I'm afraid to speak. Tears well up in my eyes at the enormity of what she's telling me.

"I made a deal with the devil, Leni. And in the end, he really did get my soul."

We both cry for a while.

I'm not sure what to do. Her hands are raw like she's scrubbed them with bleach. She sobs and says no one can forgive her.

"Won't you tell me?" I plead. "Maybe there's something we can still do, maybe we can fix it."

"No, no." She shakes her head. "No one can fix this. It's unfixable. I can't tell you, Leni, I can't. I feel sick about it. I have nightmares, I can't tell anyone."

"You can tell me, I can handle it," I tell her, echoing my mom's words in the afternoon. But this time, it doesn't work.

"No, Leni. You can't."

Natasha falls asleep eventually, but I lie awake, listening to her wheezing breaths and thinking about tainted money, curses, miracles and angels. Especially one terrible, sword-swinging, sitting-in-judgment angel, who must think we're all paltry, substandard beings.

If I look at it from his point of view, it's kind of hard to blame him.

He would already know about this, of course. He knew when he first appeared to me, which perhaps explains the less-than-gentle appearance. He's pissed off at the Kohn family and rightly so. From the way Natasha's falling apart, it must be awful, it must be the worst thing I can imagine. Which means that no matter what happens with my money, no matter what good any of us achieve during our lives, this will never be okay. I can't help stealing a glance at her, shrunken and pale as she lies near me, twitching and moaning even in her sleep.

Do I phone in an anonymous tip? Do I call the police to come arrest my sister? And tell them what, exactly? That maybe she killed someone? I don't know who or where. And I don't know for sure that she killed someone, only that whatever she did is bad enough to undo the fabric of who she is.

Natasha cries out and her eyes flutter as she's gripped by some nightmare. I lean over to shake her awake, but she settles, so I let her be. I hug my knees and rock back and forth. We can't undo what she did—whatever it is, it's irrevocable, untenable. I don't hesitate to call it the devil's work. It's all his, all the horrible ripples, all the lives ruined, it's all for his benefit. So maybe the best I can do is minimize those effects. That's what "fixing it" means. I can't reject her at her lowest point, in her time of need.

The only thing I can do is be her sister.

Chapter Nine

Whatever turmoil my private life is suffering, the first marine chemistry lab is today. I slip out of Natasha's apartment building early in the morning. There's enough time to go home, change and grab my backpack.

The air is moist and warm, like a laundry room after the dryer runs. Still, it's only in the low eighties and I appreciate the relative coolness compared with the scorcher coming. There are royal palm trees, and the smell of the salty bay is in the air. Crickets chirp and call. The hotter it is, the faster the crickets chirp, and their rate this morning is only a warm-up compared to the marathon jam sessions coming this afternoon.

At home, everyone is still asleep. I quickly get ready for school and sneak out again, no one the wiser. As I bump along the driveway on my bike, small brown lizards skitter at the sound of my approach, diving into instant camouflage under the dried oak leaves that forever need to be swept and collected. One time I startled a pygmy rattlesnake sunning itself on the driveway in the early-morning light. Ever since then, I've paid attention to the scuttling sounds on leaves because while it's usually only a lizard, sometimes it's not.

In the part of my mind that isn't completely preoccupied with angels, Natasha, the impossible task of righting an unknown wrong, the slipping sand in my hourglass (seven days, but who's counting?) and scanning for wildlife, I know this morning's lab is important to me and know what happens when you let that slip away. You sleep until ten, you stay in your pajamas for days. You drink and watch television, get fat and grow bald. So even though I'm tempted, sorely tempted, to stay home, to bang my head against the wall, or more usefully, make like a hacker and track down possibilities, I'm on my bike, heading to my local campus of Safety Harbor Community College, hoping that my lab partner will know how to run this lab, because I don't have a clue.

My lab partner. I suppress a groan as I pedal around a car stopped at a red light. I almost forgot Gavin was my partner.

I pass a small retention pond. An alligator, barely a four-footer, floats like a water-soaked log, legs splayed out underwater and only the top of its head with its protruding eyes breaking the surface. I've passed far larger alligators sunning themselves on the grassy banks of this pond. Alligators are capable of moving at speeds of up to thirty miles an hour, but they'd rather not. They get perkier around mating season but that isn't until April and even then, it's only a problem if a gator's seven feet or bigger. Of course, it's the ones you *don't* see that will get you in trouble. The few unlucky people who have been attacked, or had their dog attacked, always swear they never saw the alligator until it had them in its jaws. But when the alligator is four feet long, it's not scary, it's cute.

I cruise past the pond, dodging cars, swerving hard to avoid colliding with a wide white Cadillac that turns right from the left lane, nearly running me over. I shout a few choice words after it, knowing that even if the windows weren't rolled up tight and the golden-oldies station (Tampa Bay's most listened-to station) wasn't rocking out a top-forty hit from forty years ago, the driver still wouldn't hear me. I'll take my chances with the alligators over the snowbirds any day.

I pull up to the SHCC campus and the squat windowless building that holds the labs. The SHCC lab is well stocked and well equipped for a community college. They even have a mass spectrometer, an indispensable, expensive piece of equipment that can do everything from urinalysis to analyzing ocean water elements. The experiment we're supposed to re-create today illustrates the basics of Marcet's principle. In 1819, a Frenchman analyzed seawater from different places. He measured the six major chemical elements that make up the salt in saltwater and found that no matter how much salt there is, the ratio of the elements to each other is almost exactly the same, wherever you go in the open ocean.

This phenomenon is also called the principle of constant

proportions. I adore scientific anecdotes like this, finding out about the little links that bind us all together. Our professor obtained a sample of the Pacific Ocean for us to look at, pretty cool since it's over three thousand miles away. We have samples from Tampa Bay, of course. And since a USF research vessel recently returned from a trip to Antarctica, we even have a small vial of Weddell Sea water. What I don't know is how to operate a mass spectrometer, how to analyze the data or how long this will take. Small stuff, right?

The twenty-minute bike ride in the muggy heat has left me sweaty, grimy and probably smelly. The lab is over– air-conditioned and immediately my damp shirt turns clammy and cold as goose bumps spread across my arms and legs. I clench my teeth as I shiver, bracing myself for the unpleasant-ness to come. I won't give Gavin the satisfaction of knowing he rattles me.

Even though I'm ten minutes early, Gavin is already at one of the two long metal tables, bent over an open laptop. I'd hoped to be able to read a bit about the experiment and review the instructions before he arrived so I wouldn't look like a total moron. *Not going to happen,* I think morosely.

He glances up when he hears the door open. He's filled out in past years, his shoulders broader; he's grown into his height. I hate to admit it, he's intimidating in his faded gray shirt and cargo shorts. In a way that most science geeks don't, he looks tough. Maybe it's the C-shaped scar on his forearm that wasn't there when I knew him two years ago. His hair is a lot shorter than it used to be, when he wore it long and loose like a slacker rock star. It looks better short. He hasn't shaved this morning, giving him that scruffy outlaw look.

My chin tilts up in automatic challenge as I wait for him to say something about this reunion. But he only nods hello and goes back to work. It throws me off balance but after a moment, I decide he's right. This isn't the time and frankly, there's nothing to revisit. He was someone who went to my high school a few years ago. He's my lab partner now, and that's it. No need to make more of it. I put him out of my mind and set my bag at the other metal table.

The overhead fluorescent lights make the whole room seem like it's slightly glowing. The TA has already set up the instrument and stepped out, meaning we're alone in the narrow room. There's a sink and an eye-wash station, while several clear fiberglass hoods cover work spaces to protect ongoing experiments.

The mass spectrometer is plugged in on one wide, cleared counter. It doesn't look like much, a beige box, some cables—it could be a fancy printer.

Though the TA hasn't come back yet, I head over to the prep area and line up our samples, the glass slides, the pipettes. Gavin watches me for a moment before stepping next to me and helping finish the prep, his movements quick and precise.

"Have you ever used one of these?" he asks, not looking at me.

"No. I've read about them, though." I can hear the defensiveness in my voice and I slide my gaze over to him, ready for a fight.

"So you'll be the PI today, cool?"

Letting me be the principal investigator means we run the lab at my pace, on my terms.

"Yeah." I try not to sound surprised at this generous gesture. "Thanks."

He finally looks over at me and smiles a small, pleased smile at my reaction. "I figured you might want to get your hands wet." His voice has a slight southern drawl to it that I'd almost forgotten. He doesn't sound nervous like I do.

"It's too early for puns."

He grins. "It's never too early."

I step up to the $100,000 beast and begin running through the steps the lab overview lists. Gavin is certainly in a better mood this morning than he was in class. I wonder at the change but figure it has nothing to do with me.

Using pipettes, we place a drop of seawater on various small glass slides for the mass spectrometer to analyze.

He jots down the numbers as the computer pulls them up. I came fully prepared that he would either hog the entire experiment and not let me do anything, nastily condescending the entire time, or the flip side, do nothing and have me do all the work (which I'd prefer, given a choice). But instead, he's the perfect lab partner. Darn it.

The TA comes in at some point. Bearded and pale, he tells us he's a PhD candidate at USF. I fill in the rest: he's here to make a few extra bucks. The only thing he really cares about is that we don't cause any permanent damage to the lab equipment. He watches our progress for a bit. What he sees must reassure him that the machine is in safe hands because he's soon scribbling in a journal and writing complex equations with a Sharpie on the clear plastic doors of the hoods that vent toxic chemicals.

We complete the experiment, clean up, and then enter data in the Results section of our lab report. I lean back on my metal stool and smile.

"You're not a bad lab partner," I say.

"I like how you leave *You're not nearly as big a jerk as I thought you would be* hanging in the air."

"It was a pleasant surprise," I say blandly.

He grins at my response, and my stomach foolishly flips. *Stop!* I command my thoughts. *Do not go there.*

"I took some college classes when I was in high school, before, you know . . ." Before he was arrested and sent to juvie. Yeah, I know. "There was always some jerk who got a thrill from making me feel young and stupid." He zips up his bag and then nails me with a look. "I always swore that when I had a high schooler in class with me, I'd be their lab partner and I wouldn't be that way."

For a moment, I don't know what to say.

I'm nobody's charity case. "Now you can cross that vow off your to-do list," I say.

"Do you want to get a coffee and finish the conclusion?" he offers.

"No thanks. You know, I always swore that if I had a college student as my lab partner I'd show him high schoolers are bright and hardworking and don't need anyone holding their hands to get their work done," I say sweetly.

He pauses in surprise and quickly suppresses a smile. "Great, then you'll finish up writing the conclusion? 'Preciate it, Leni."

He doesn't wait for a clever retort, just says "bye" and lopes out of the lab, his long legs eating up space and leaving me quickly behind, my weak "bye" hanging in the cool air.

One: How did he know he'd get me as his lab partner when he signed up first?

Two: What is Gavin doing back in St. Petersburg?

Which leads me nicely to question three: What is a guy who took a bunch of college classes in high school, who should be a sophomore at Tech, doing at SHCC? At the very least, he should be taking classes at USF. Instead, he's at a community college taking a course he probably aced years ago.

Whatever Gavin might be, he isn't stupid.

Which means he has a reason for doing this. But the answer to that one completely eludes me.

Chapter Ten

Sofia, one of three girls who work part-time at Steeped, is there when I arrive.

"Is Natasha in?" I ask, heading to the back office.

"Just left." Sofia's a college student majoring in communications. With her Cuban heritage showing in her flawless caramel skin, coal-black eyes and gorgeous hair, she seems made for television, but her dream job is to work for NPR. She volunteers at our local station, and every once in a while she helps out on a story.

The office door's locked.

"Did she say when she'd be back?"

Sofia pauses, thinking about it.

"No," she finally says. "She said she'd be back before my shift ended. And I'm on until nine." There's an open textbook and a highlighter on the counter, and while she doesn't sound annoyed at the questions, she must want to keep studying while the tea shop is temporarily quiet and empty.

"Did she seem okay?"

She looks up from her book and studies me for a second. Then she shrugs. "I guess so," she says. "She seemed in a hurry, kind of stressed, but normal."

"Oh. All right, then."

Sofia looks like she wants to ask me something, but then she returns to studying. I slouch over to a corner table by an outlet. I am not a procrastinator by nature and I imagine Michael hovering behind me, fingers tapping impatiently. Squirming, I open my laptop, thinking I'll look into . . . what? Where can I even start? I feel twitchy with the need to do something but I still don't know what to do about Natasha's confession. Sofia's highlighting a long passage in her textbook. And what exactly can I do to prepare for this? Research angel encounters? Read blogs about the devil? I promised to fix it, but how can I fix a deal made with the devil by my sister? How can I fix my parents' winning the lottery and blowing nearly all of it? I tend to grind my teeth when I'm annoyed and the sound of it snaps me out of my brewing tempest.

Fine, I think. *Leave it alone and try to think outside the box.*

Seeing Sofia study reminds me that I have homework of my own. I need to enter the lab results and write my conclusion. Glad to have something constructive to do, I decide to finish the lab report and turn it in early, my favorite way to turn in an assignment.

But when Google's open-ended, nearly blank search page

winks at me, I'm suddenly inspired to investigate a different mystery, one that seems a lot less frightening. Without a shred of conscience, I Google one Gavin Armand. It only takes a few seconds to narrow down the search, weeding out a psychologist who cowrote a paper on kleptomania and a country music artist whose first album is selling poorly on iTunes. My Gavin Armand (and oh, since when had I come to think of him as *mine?*) shows up on the second page of results. I click on the link for an article in a college newspaper. Gavin Armand was a student at Tech, expelled on honor charges. I read the article in disbelief.

> While Armand continues to deny the charges against him, and despite the many testimonials in his defense, the honor committee has ruled that overwhelming evidence conclusively proves a major honor violation was committed. "There was no way he was telling the truth," said one student panel member, who asked to remain anonymous. "He seems like a great guy and a lot of people like him, but the facts are pretty obvious. He was the first person in his class to check out the book, and afterward the chapter on code-breaking that everyone needed to complete the assignment was cut out. He must have thought cutting it out would cause the other students to fail, but instead he was caught."
>
> Armand has decided not to appeal the ruling. He is the third student expelled from Tech on honor violations this year.

On the one hand, the article explains why he's back here in Florida, why he's at SHCC instead of USF.

But it doesn't explain what the heck happened. How could someone so smart, a genius-jerk, think he would get away with cutting a mandatory reading out of a book that no one else had read yet? You'd have to be a moron, and whatever else Gavin is, moron isn't one of them. I wonder why no one brought that up, that he's too smart to do something so stupid.

I wonder why he didn't fight to clear his name. I would have thought, after juvie, he'd have done anything to protect his future. And how did he go from juvie to Tech in the first place?

The silver bell on the front door jingles as a middle-aged woman in a short skirt and bright beaded top enters the shop. Sofia pushes her book aside and looks up with a smile. I tune out their chatter. But soon the bell's ringing frequently and the counter begins crowding with customers waiting to put in an order. I save the article to study later and head behind the counter to help.

"Thanks, Leni." Sofia smiles over her shoulder as she brews two teas. "I'll brew, you take orders, okay?"

I tie an apron on and turn to the next person in line.

An hour passes in a whirl of orders and change and credit-card receipts. Lots of iced drinks and afternoon pick-me-ups. I recommend some drinks and talk up the week's special: iced Moroccan mint tea and chocolate chip cookies. I keep expecting to see Natasha hurrying in to help out with the afternoon rush like she always does, and the longer she stays away, the more uneasy I grow.

After my parents won the lottery, they told us that Natasha and I both had to wait until we were eighteen before we could spend our money. For Natasha, it meant waiting a year. During that year, she planned out exactly what to do with the money. She had always wanted her own shop, and so for a year she searched out the perfect location, signed up for business classes at the community college, and attended the chamber of commerce's monthly meetings as she finished high school. We were sure that as soon as she had her birthday she'd run out and open a store. But she didn't. After she turned eighteen and graduated from high school, she spent the next year and a half traveling to India, Japan and Great Britain to learn about tea. She visited plantations, factories and the world's greatest tearooms. Everywhere she went, she charmed the people she met. Such a young girl, so focused, so rich. She received advice and tips from the best, and secured shipments that other tea shops could only covet. All the obsession she'd poured into Emmett, she turned to the shop. Privately, we all believed she'd grow tired of it. It was so much work, most of it tedious. It hardly seemed possible that the impulsive, temperamental girl we'd all endured would be a good businesswoman. But she was. She opened the store two months after her twentieth birthday, and before the year was up, the store was profitable. By her next birthday, it had won Best of the Bay.

I enter two orders and tuck the bills into the register drawer.

Whatever drama Natasha had going on in her life—and with Natasha, you could always count on the fact that there would be drama—she always kept it out of the shop. She had completely compartmentalized her life. As bad as she looked last night, it's her absence now that really worries me.

In the inexplicable ways of herd thinking, the sudden rush is over and the shop is deserted again. If I ended up studying sociology, I'd write a thesis on it: "Humans and Wildebeests: Common Genetic Heritage and Herd Instincts."

I smile at the thought and Sofia, seeing the smile, mistakes it.

"I'm glad you're in a better mood," she says. "You seemed pretty pissed off when you came in."

"What?"

"You don't have to talk about it if you don't want," she says, smirking because, of course, she is a budding journalist and notices things like moody high schoolers. "But I'm the same way—being busy is so much better than brooding. Want to talk about it?"

I actually consider telling Sofia that Natasha made a deal with the devil, that an angel came to me while I was meditating. That I have seven freaking days to fix everything, even though I don't even know what "everything" is, let alone how to fix it. And maybe God did create the entire world in seven days, but I'm not God and I don't know what to do. And I want to tell her all about it, not because she'll be able to help but because I hate carrying this huge secret around. For a split second, I imagine how good it would feel to tell her this, and it takes another instant to imagine her response.

So even with all her winning ways, I'm not telling her the real reason I'm "pissed off" and "brooding." Of course, I have other issues and maybe she'll have insight on any number of things.

"When something doesn't make sense . . . if you find out

something about someone that doesn't fit, what do you do about it?" I gesture at her textbook pushed to the side. "I mean, as a reporter." Here's a tip: When avoiding scrutiny, always answer a question with a question. Vaguely.

She shoots me an appraising look.

"It's not a juicy story," I assure her. "There's this guy in my marine chem class at SHCC." I pronounce it "shek." "I used to go to high school with him, actually. He's sending mixed signals."

"Oooh, Leni's got a boyfriend," she teases.

"No, I mean, he's back in town and he was supposed to be away at college. It doesn't make sense."

"I'll tell you what my professors always tell us in class." I lean in, ready for pearls of wisdom. "When something doesn't make sense, follow it. Dig deeper. And whenever possible, go straight to the source."

I picture walking up to Gavin, looking (way up) into his eyes and digging into why he didn't fight the honor charges leveled against him.

"That's not helpful," I accuse. "Your professors suck."

She laughs like I meant her to.

"I'll be sure to tell my Pulitzer-winning professor you feel that way." She wipes the counter in careful, efficient strokes.

"They give those out like candy these days."

"I heard that," she breathes, wide-eyed. "It's such a scandal."

I snigger as I go to our self-service cart, refill the milk canister and clean up smeared honey and glittering crystals of spilled sugar.

"Seriously, though," she says. "Going to the source doesn't

mean confrontation. That rarely works anyway. You just need to give the person who's at the center of it all a chance to speak for themselves. Let them show you what the view looks like from their side of the story." She lets it sink in. "If it made the news, that means it's haunting them. And if it's haunting them, then they're itching for a chance to talk about it with someone who'll listen. So listen, don't judge. That's another thing my idiot, Pulitzer-winning professor says a lot."

I humph, as if what she says still doesn't make sense, except it does. It makes a lot of sense. I know I'd love to talk about my news. If I thought for a moment someone would listen without judging, I'd spill everything.

Sofia returns to studying and I head back to my laptop to work on my lab report, mulling over her advice. And how it can apply to more than Gavin's mystery.

R u alive? I text Natasha.

She texts back almost immediately. Unfortunately.

Wanna talk?

No!

As I head home, pushing my bike and fighting the conclusion I keep arriving to, I return to the thought I had when I first saw Natasha at the shop three days ago.

This isn't a problem money can fix.

The tea-shop job started as a desperate measure to get some money. After budget cuts suddenly meant her professor couldn't pay for a student researcher anymore, Sofia had a moment of real panic. Her mom couldn't step in and fill that five-thousand-dollar gap—Phil had lost his job again and her mom needed to pick up a couple of extra shifts at the hospital to keep up with mortgage payments. And NPR, God love them, thought they were doing her a favor letting her intern for free. It wasn't fair to blame them, she knew, but with the internship taking fifteen hours a week, and classes and homework, she wasn't left with many options for a part-time job. Her mom suggested, this time with bite, that Sofia switch majors. A nursing career was reliable, with good pay and a flexible schedule. "You're starting to get a taste of what life can be like, scrambling for money. Trust me, you don't want to go down there."

Sofia tried to imagine life as a nurse. Drawing blood, changing vomit-stained sheets, taking orders from arrogant doctors, and she shuddered at the thought of that misery stretching out for years to come. What was the point of living if you didn't fight for your dreams? How could she give up on them at age twenty? Her mom had had a rough time, no doubt about it: single mom, two worthless husbands; it's not that Sofia didn't understand where she was coming from. Her mom's nursing career was the only thing that kept them off food stamps and in their condo. Still, it was beyond depressing to imagine living her mom's life.

Sofia had met Natasha during an NPR fund-raiser and had thought she was kind of a bitch, but one with style. When Sofia ran into her a couple of days after the budget cuts, they started chatting and the next thing she knew, Sofia was crying and Natasha, listening with such kindness, gave her a tissue and a job offer with flexible hours and surprisingly good pay. It turned out that Natasha was a pretty great boss as long as you didn't take her mood swings personally. Natasha had taken Sofia's suggestions of serving Taiwanese bubble tea on the weekends and offering weekly tea and dessert pairings. As if she knew, or guessed, the tight budget Sofia kept herself on, Natasha always sent her home with the leftover baked goods at the end of the day. Sofia would freeze them and defrost a muffin each morning for breakfast, and sometimes have one for lunch too. It made a difference.

It was obvious that something was wrong when Natasha came into the store today. Natasha always had this special aura about her. If Sofia had to describe her for a radio audience, she would say that shop owner Natasha Kohn looked like the kind of person good things happened to, not because she was lucky, but because she was extraordinary. Except Sofia would never actually say that on the radio because it would sound like she had a girl crush on Natasha. Which, okay, maybe she did, but that's not something you shared with your radio listeners.

Today, though, Natasha looked gray and defeated. Like her aura had sprung a leak and all her special passion, that shimmering quality that made people turn their head when she walked by, was gone. Sofia told her she needed to go home, have some chicken soup, get some rest. Natasha didn't want to leave her in the lurch during the afternoon rush, but Sofia practically pushed her out the door. As Natasha finally headed out, looking weary and sad, she said to tell anyone who came looking for her that she was at home and could be reached on her cell.

Sofia debated telling Leni this, but Leni looked like a hound dog trying to catch a scent on the wind. Her inquisitive face scrunched with suspicion and worry, her mouth twisting when she asked about Natasha, as if the very name left a bad taste. Impulsively Sofia *felt like covering for Natasha. To give her the space she so clearly needed.*

Whatever was wrong with Natasha, it wasn't something Leni could fix. Sofia liked Leni well enough, but you didn't have to be a genius to see that the sisters didn't mix well on the best of days. And something about the way Natasha looked told Sofia that this was close to the worst day Natasha had ever had.

It was a small thing to lead Leni off Natasha, to get her thinking about something else. But like getting free muffins, sometimes every little thing helped.

Chapter Eleven

The phone rings as I struggle to lock the front door behind me. Metal fixtures don't do well in the salty air, and ours have started to corrode. I could ignore it like my parents always do, but some weird compulsion against unanswered calls has me rushing up the stairs to answer the hall phone.

It's a woman asking for my mom.

"She's not here."

"Please tell her Spa Mystique called to confirm her appointment on Tuesday at ten."

My mom has made an appointment at St. Petersburg's most exclusive medi-spa days before my birthday? With a sinking heart, I realize this means she's already spending the money she believes is coming her way.

"I can't confirm that," I finally say.

"Excuse me?" the receptionist asks in surprise.

"She won't be able to make it."

"I see," she says, coolly professional. "Please tell her to call back and reschedule."

"No."

"What?" The polite customer voice is gone.

"Yeah. She forgot to tell you. We're broke." Then I hang up.

I kick the wall and glare at the phone. What else has my mom already charged, knowing that by the time the credit-card bill arrives, the money will be hers? The appointment with Spa Mystique proves that another million dollars won't fix anything. It'll prolong the inevitable.

Zaydie, my mom's dad, was a Holocaust survivor. He had grown up in a wealthy German family. Within four years of the Nazis' taking power, the family lost everything. By the time Zaydie was my age, he'd gone from a pampered little boy with servants and horses to a penniless orphan, lucky to be alive.

He never talked much about that time of his life, not even to my mom, except that he always said, "You never know what life has waiting for you around the corner, so enjoy what you have while you have it."

Maybe my mom felt the lottery money was cosmic retribution, divine justice. Maybe she felt this was a rightful inheritance, or maybe there was a *carpe diem* thing going on and both my parents wanted to have fun while they still could. As long as the money lasted. Either way, this appointment means she hasn't changed her basic view that if money's around, you spend it.

I pound my head softly against the wall cursing under my breath.

I imagine telling my parents I've changed my mind. *You're not good with money and I'll spend this trust fund you gave me way better than you will.*

I might as well drive a knife in their back.

And you're not a good daughter, they'll say, and they'll be right. *You took what we gave you when times were good and now that we need your help, you're out the door with a million bucks.*

Or how about I tell them that an angel told me to spend the money. That the devil rigged the lotto so Dad would win, and that Natasha had to do something awful seven years later. Yeah. Then all the trust-fund money would go to pay for my psychiatric bills at the asylum.

I kick the wall again.

"The wallpaper does suck but that's not the best way to remove it."

I scream, and whirl to see Eddie at the top of the stairs looking at me with interest. He's wearing the same shirt he wore yesterday, a stained and faded Red Cross blood-drive giveaway from eight years ago. It's a generic XL and a little tight around his gut. He hasn't shaved this morning or showered, from the looks of his hair.

"What are you doing here?" I demand, flustered and embarrassed. "I haven't seen you upstairs in years."

"Har, har. I heard the sounds of a fight. Figured you were using kung fu on an intruder."

"You came to help?"

"I came to cheer you on, babe," he says, and I can't help smiling back at the impish look on his face. "Been a while since I've been to an MMA fight."

"Thanks for the vote of confidence." But my smile wobbles at the thought of how misplaced that confidence is.

"What's wrong, kid?" he asks. "You haven't been yourself lately."

"You noticed?" I really didn't think Eddie noticed much of anything besides what was on TV or his plate.

"Yeah, we all did. You and Natasha had a fight? Neither one of you has been acting right since she came back from visiting her tattooed menace in Tennessee."

"It wasn't Emmett's fault," I say automatically.

"Whatever." Eddie gives me a funny look. "Come down-stairs, I can't stand it up here." Before turning away, he sneers in disgust at the beige-and-gold fleur-de-lis wallpaper that covers the hallway. I follow his bulk down the stairs to the den, with its hunter-green silk wallpaper that the decorator insisted would re-create an English-style club. She was wrong. There's a fake mounted buck's head (I wouldn't let them put in a real one); bookcases that hold volumes that look like gold-tooled, leather-bound classics but are actually made of hollow plastic; and the infamous wood floor that buckles in several places. Perpetually dark and gloomy, it's my least favorite room in the whole awful house. The large flat-screen TV's on, like always, but at least Eddie clicks it to mute as he sinks heavily into the big leather recliner. From Eddie, it's a gesture of extreme consideration and it means he's planning on a serious conversation. If this turns into a sex-ed talk, I'm bolting out of my chair.

"I know you have a lot on your plate, Leni," he begins gravely, after shifting the recliner so that his legs are propped up. "High school is"—he searches for the right words—"it's . . . it's a time when you feel like every decision you make is going to shape the rest of your life."

I lean against the armrest of the matching leather couch, but shift my weight to the balls of my feet, ready to flee the instant this conversation turns to "strong feelings" and/or "contraceptives."

"You've got this trust-fund issue to deal with. If you're unhappy because of the money," he says, "then I want to give you some advice."

It isn't sex ed, but I still brace myself for the suggestion he will be compelled to make: give the money to Mom and Dad. Or heck, maybe he'll say I should hand it over to him since he hasn't partied in four years. Then I can add Eddie to the list of family members who hate me. In fact, given that Natasha has been avoiding me like the plague, maybe Eddie would make it a full house.

The sad thing is that when Eddie was in high school, I thought he was the coolest, smartest, best big brother in the world. When Natasha picked on me, I always ran to Eddie. Now it's like someone performed a partial lobotomy on him. My handsome, kind, ruddy older brother has turned into this gray, slovenly, gluttonous lump. Even his hands have gotten fat, with thick sausage fingers—nothing like the once strong, capable hands that, like my dad's, could make broken things work again.

But even as I'm cataloging all the aspects of his ruin, Eddie eyes me meaningfully. His eyes, the exact same shade as my own, have an alert look that catches me off guard. I haven't seen anything like it in a while.

"It's a joke, kid," he says. "You're being robbed of the best experience of your life."

It takes me a second to realize what he's saying.

"You think I should keep the money?" I squeak in surprise.

"Hell, yes, you should keep the money. It's yours!"

"But Mom and Dad need it," I splutter. "Look around! This place is falling apart."

"Forget about that," Eddie says. "Think about what you want most in the world, Leni. Picture it." His hands make a frame. "Your money can buy that. Can you really tell me that what you want most in the world is for Mom and Dad to keep living in this piece-of-shit mansion?"

"I've hated this place from the day we moved in!" I take a deep breath and force myself to stop yelling. "That's not what giving them the money is for. It's for taking care of my parents, who always took care of me."

Eddie shakes his head before I even finish.

"You only get a chance like this once in your life. Use it up and it's gone." I shiver at his ominous tone. "A million dollars, Leni." He leans forward and grabs my arm. His palms are clammy and damp with sweat. I flinch and instinctively tug my arm but he holds on, fingers squeezing tightly. "Do you know what I would give to have a million dollars again?" He sucks in his lip and his eyes blaze. "I would give anything to have another chance. It's the most amazing feeling in the world. Everywhere you go, anything you see, it's yours if you want it.

You have friends. You're smart. You're funny. You're hot. You're the center of the universe." He leans way too close and the musty, cottony smell of his stale breath wafts over me.

I yank my arm out of his grip, disgust crossing my face. He sees it and that crazy light fades. He leans back in his recliner, as if in a giant cradle.

"I probably didn't spend my money in the smartest way, not like Natasha with her freakin' tea shop. But I wouldn't trade those two years I had for anything."

"Except maybe another million dollars," I say, only half-kidding.

"Yeah, there's that." Rueful self-awareness flashes by. He's still there, the brother I remember from childhood. I want to ask him more, about why he doesn't finish his degree, why he doesn't do anything, not even play recreational baseball like he used to. Then the TV flickers and his eyes shift, catching an instant replay of some awesome catch. His attention drifts to the game, and his hand, almost of its own volition, slides toward the remote control. This surprising window of candor and clarity has closed as quickly and unexpectedly as it opened. But before he clicks the sound back on, before he turns away and tunes in and leaves me to my own devices, Eddie has one last piece of advice to give.

"We all got the chance to feel like kings, to feel like a god," he says as his green eyes, bloodshot and moist, drift toward the glowing screen. "Don't give them your money, only to resent them for the rest of your life." Then he settles back with a small belch and turns the volume up.

The Rays are tied at the bottom of the sixth and Eddie, with his insights and regrets and touch of madness, is self-medicating again. His face is slack, his eyes dull and fixed on the screen.

He might as well be in a different country, he is that far gone from me.

Chapter Twelve

I wake up Saturday morning feeling weird and achy. Six days until my birthday and my head feels somewhere between a headache and vertigo. My stomach turns in a slow, nasty way that bodes badly for a morning spent under the brutal sun. My room is already hot and stuffy, the ceiling fan only stirring the soup, not cooling it.

Weeks earlier, before classes started, I signed up to join a group of students from SHCC for a beach cleanup. It sounded like a great project and a good way to meet students outside class. Now it sounds awful. I'm no closer than I was on Wednesday to figuring out what to do. Time is running short. The only thing that has me leaving my bed is the fact that staying at home is worse than heading out. Maybe going back to the beach will bring some brilliant solution. A girl can hope, right?

I smear on a palmful of sunscreen and head downstairs. Feeling a little better after toast and jelly, I pack a thermos of ice water and a towel in my backpack. My parents aren't up yet and no one sees Eddie until late afternoon. I leave a note on the counter and depart the silent house.

A large van idles in front of the library as it waits for students to board, something that always annoys me. Idling engines produce more pollution per minute than driving. If people turned off their cars when they weren't driving, they'd save gasoline as well as wear and tear on their cars. It's ironic that students off to clean the beach are polluting the air.

I'm early, so I sit on the steps leading up to the library and rest my head on my arms. The sun bakes my back and cooks my headache. I'm clearly failing at fixing the mess my family's in, and I know that the powers that be are disappointed. As I sit there, I grow angry at the idling van. There's no one even in the van, so I open the door and switch off the ignition. Almost as soon as the engine is cut, the inside of the van begins heating up. I return to my spot on the steps and put my head down in my lap, my headache no better.

"Are you coming?" a girl asks. "The van's about to leave."

To my surprise, the sidewalk and steps are deserted. Everyone has boarded the van, which is now idling again. I rub my temple and wince.

"Yeah," I say, rising.

She gives me a funny look, another conquest of my infamous charm. As she heads over to the van, I follow her, shuffling my feet like an old woman.

By the time I board the van, almost all the bench seats are

taken. For a moment, it looks like I'll have to turn around and disembark and I feel speared by simultaneous relief and disappointment.

"Leni," someone calls out. "There's room back here."

A hand waves from the back. It's the girl from marine chemistry class, the one on her third major, wearing a vintage-looking Lucky Charms shirt. She scoots over to make room, then nudges me and rolls her eyes, pointing to someone behind us.

"He's such a hottie," she murmurs in my ear.

Even before swiveling to take a look, I already know there's only one person who evokes such a response. With a sinking heart, I see Gavin with his earbuds in, busy tapping at a tiny screen, oblivious to the stares he's getting. He has a backpack on the seat next to him. He doesn't notice my glance.

I turn back to Lucky Charms, smiling weakly. The morning's outing is looking less and less likely to be pleasant.

"We're lab partners now," I whisper, as if he can hear.

"Oh God, lucky you!"

I shrug and then wince at the blade of agony this sends through my brain. "You wouldn't have any Advil, would you?"

She's instantly solicitous and digs through her small backpack like a busy squirrel. "I usually do," she says, her head half-buried in the bag. "I get killer cramps during my period. But I think I took the last two a week ago. I'm so sorry. You look miserable."

"It's okay," I say, happy that we're not talking about Gavin. "I'm sure it'll pass. I don't usually get headaches."

She pats my hand and then kindly falls quiet. We both lean

back and watch the bay sparkle in the morning sunlight. The little flickers of light, bright as flares, should make my headache worse, but they're oddly soothing. There and gone, they look like fairy dust, powerful and ephemeral. Lucky Charms dozes off, I really need to learn her name. I must doze too, because I wake with a start as I realize that people are getting off the bus. I shake my seatmate awake. She looks a bit flustered and disoriented.

"Don't worry," I say, because she's furtively wiping her mouth like she might have drooled. "I fell asleep too. We just got here."

She smiles tentatively. I pat her leg. "Let's get to work, huh?"

"Yay," she says weakly. "Why did I think this was a good idea, again?"

As I step down, the sun and heat are like a brick wall, a physical presence and a shock after the blasting air-conditioning in the van. That beloved beach smell of salt, seaweed and decomposing sea life brings a small smile to my face. I love this place. Behind me, Lucky Charms staggers a bit at the heat. As the last of the students disembark, Gavin makes his way down. He nods when our eyes meet but doesn't seem surprised. Maybe he noticed me on the van after all. People split into teams, and the driver, a volunteer with Keep Pinellas Beautiful, distributes large trash bags and rubber gloves. There are a few trash grabbers, long sticks with pincers on the end so you don't have to touch things or keep bending over, but the people sitting at the front of the van have already snagged those. I take two large bags, figuring that's all I'll be able to carry, and a pair of rubber gloves, which I shove into the waistband of my shorts to use later. I don't bother trying to partner up with anyone. Lucky Charms is chatting with a group of people she knows, her high energy back in place.

The guy who organized this excursion explains the basics and then everyone scatters, spreading across the beautiful expanse of powder-fine sand. I walk fast to gain distance between me and the rest of the students before really taking in the view. The dark blue-green of the Gulf spreads out like Neptune's blanket. Under the brutal sun, the winking water is inviting. In July and August, the water can get so warm it's like standing in a great pool of bathwater, with no temperature difference between the air and the sea. But by mid-September, the water's cooled off enough to be refreshing. It's the end of the stingray migration as well. During the summer, they like to lie motionless, half-covered with sand, under the shallow water of the Gulf. You have to enter the water with "the stingray shuffle," dragging your feet so that stingrays feel the vibrations and scoot away, and so that you don't step on one. If you do step down on a stingray, it'll whip up its barb and sting you, which, while not life-threatening, is extremely painful. I've had a couple of friends who were stung; they spent a miserable afternoon shivering with the reaction. We get jellyfish too, of course, some worse than others. If it's a moon jellyfish, which has very short tentacles, or a comb jelly, which isn't even a true jellyfish, then I don't hesitate to head in for a swim. If it's a sea nettle, or worse, a Portuguese man-of-war, I won't go in at all. I once saw a woman screaming on the beach as several people huddled around her, trying to help. Someone said she'd been stung by a man-of-war, and the lifeguard cleared the beach of swimmers. A Portuguese man-of-war can send an adult to the hospital and its barbed tentacles can stretch an average of thirty feet behind them.

Scraggy sand dunes, with their clinging sea grapes and droopy sea oats hanging on for dear life, edge the beach. This beach is one of the few that isn't built up with condos and houses. Even so, there are plastic bottles, a single black rubber flip-flop, faded beer cans, a cloud of torn plastic bags, and various other flotsam left by that most invasive and destructive animal of all. Us.

I walk farther and farther away from the main group, feeling better as I leave them behind, the breeze plays softly with my hair and the sandpipers scatter every time I draw near. I pick up trash, shove it in my bag. The bay doesn't get many breakers, so the lap of little waves is like a soft heartbeat. A line of crushed shells snakes along the edge of the surf but I stay away, knowing I wouldn't be able to resist picking through them for pretty treasures—Florida fighting conch, baby's ear, giant heart cockle, angel wing, even fossilized shark teeth. It's the closest I've been to relaxed since Natasha laid her bomb on me.

I catch a glimpse of a shiny black dorsal fin a hundred yards offshore. Before I even form the thought *Dolphin!* there's another one and another. It's a large pod, seven, maybe eight dolphins. For some reason, I think about my dolphin, the one my parents bought me years ago. She's not one of them, of course. She was never released back into the wild, but seeing these wild dolphins, I'm struck by a deep longing to see her again, to make sure she's okay.

Impulsively I kick off my sandals and pull off my shirt. My nylon shorts will dry fast and my blue sports bra covers more than most bikinis. Then I race through the surf, splashing water, and dive headfirst as soon as the water's past my knees. The instant my head goes under, I can hear their clicks and squeaks.

I tread water a careful twenty feet away from them, hardly daring to breathe. Dolphins are curious, though, and two sleek, powerful creatures, bigger than me, stronger, and masters of their element, swim over and check me out. They glide by so smoothly, so fast, that the primitive part of my brain suddenly remembers that these beloved creatures are predators. With teeth clenched, I tread water, keeping my head above the waterline, poised between glee and terror. Their blue-gray skin, smooth as plastic, blends with the clear green water. As one draws near, I stretch out my hand and touch it on the flank, feeling its surprisingly hard, rubbery body before it disappears under the water and reappears yards away. Its bright eyes seem to laugh at me, at the silly daring touch. I laugh out loud. It slips underwater, and bobs up again more yards away, back with its pod.

Once I swim to shore, I can't stop laughing.

My heart racing with adrenaline, I throw myself down on the sand, delight and sheer joy zinging through every joint, and fizzing fits of giggles overtake me. I wish there were someone here with me to feel this.

Eventually I brush off the sand and pull my shirt over my sopping wet bra. I'm happy and relaxed, my weird headache gone, the nausea gone, my body so tingly from the water, the sand and the burning hot sun that it takes me a while to realize I'm not alone.

His presence reveals itself slowly but with growing intensity, prickling along my skin like electricity.

I instinctively stand, knowing I need to brace myself.

"Oh," I say softly. "Oh. Oh." And then feeling like I have to say something, I whisper, "You're back."

Whatever doubts I managed to invent since his last visit— the sad loneliness—vanish with a soundless *poof.* Because Michael is back and he is with me. There is no terrible pain this time, no physical attack, but the intensity of his presence, growing by the second, skates right along the line of pain. The prickling heat grows hotter. My skin is on fire.

I turn my face straight into the blinding hot sun because he is there, and everywhere, and nowhere, and I don't know what else to do. I can't run from this so I throw myself into his punishing inferno. Maybe it hurt so much last time because I fought it, because I was unprepared. My molecules incinerate and scatter to the winds, the assumption of me gone. Terrifying. Thrilling. I close my eyes against the impossible glare and see a wash of red behind my lids.

We never left you, the angel says to me. He is angry and kind, impatient and loving. My knees buckle as he booms in my head, and I dimly feel the scorching sand, like granules of fire, my arms and legs burning in a weird echo of the burning pain already there. *We're always with you.* A promise. A threat.

I try to hold on to the sound of his voice, though it is sound-less. I try to hold on to that voice full of love and power, forgiveness and fury. How enraging for a powerful creature like him to deal with a weakling like me. His voice is like holding molten lead, so hot it almost feels cold as it slips and burns through my fingers. A blazing heat that doesn't consume. I am nothing before him.

He speaks. I listen.

Lenore, he says, and the way he says my name is the way a mother calls for her little babe and the way an enraged father bellows for a naughty child. The tender love is there, as is the exasperation, and the patience strained to the point of snapping. *Lenore, make right what has been set wrong. Choose to heal old wounds.*

I'm not quite lucid enough to speak; even forming coherent thoughts is hard. I'm trying so hard to listen. To remember every word he says.

The one who was wronged will come to you, he says in a voice that is prophetic and infuriatingly vague. *Who is it?* I want to scream. *What am I supposed to do?*

Fix it, he booms.

My mind spins under the assault. So much on the line. So much up to me.

We are always with you, he says. Which is great. But also: *Do not fail us.* Which frightens me.

The careful balance I struggle for wobbles. It is too much. I fight the vortex below me, the hanging sword above; I must keep my focus. But the stack of balanced cups and spinning plates that is my concentration teeters. I have time to gasp in fear. Then it all comes crashing down. I catch a sense of

Michael's impatience, the stunning frustration of dealing with a substandard minion, before I lose any sense of meaning in his words or the ability to track what he is saying. I'm lying at the bottom of the ocean looking up at a whirlpool. Then the whirlpool closes in over me and everything goes dark.

Chapter Thirteen

"Leni! Leni!" Someone calls my name.

I should say something.

"Leni!" The voice is full of concern. "Leni!"

Strong hands lift my head and lay it on a hard lap. The bright red of the sun's glare behind my eyes vanishes into lovely darkness. Something cold and wet dribbles on my face and makes me gasp, which causes me to breathe in water. I sputter, sitting up too quickly, only to knock into something hard.

"Oh!" I cry out and grab my forehead.

There's an echoing cry and the shade is gone. As my eyes pop open, the bright glare of the sun slaps my eyeballs.

I pitch sideways, clutching my eyes, and land with my face in the burning hot sand.

"Ack!" I say with a mouthful of grit. Blinking against the bright glare, I turn to face my bumbling rescuer.

"What the hell are you on?" Gavin says.

Of all people on this earth. Why Gavin?

I'm reeling from my visit, from the knock on the head. I touch my forehead gently and feel a lump rising. I'm utterly unprepared for a showdown. Gavin sits less than a foot away and rubs his mouth gingerly.

As he lowers his hand, I can see that I clocked him good.

"You're bleeding," I say in a small voice.

He shoots me an annoyed look. Then he reaches for his canteen, takes a swig, swishes and spits in the sand.

"Are you okay?" he asks after a significant pause. He clearly expects some great explanation about what just happened. Something along the lines of epileptic seizure or diabetic coma. An Ecstasy tablet gone bad. Something that makes sense.

I don't answer.

"I saw you collapse," he accuses. "It scared the crap out of me."

I don't want to talk. Michael's words are slipping away so quickly I can almost see them blowing away. Leaving with them is my understanding of what I'm supposed to do. I don't want to talk to Gavin about this. Especially not Gavin. Still woozy from my encounter, my head spins as I try to stand, and I stumble back against him. He catches me and eases me down to the sand. Though weak and dizzy, I still notice that his chest is broad and solid.

"It's the heat," I lie, poorly, rubbing my throbbing temples.

"Bull," he says, though he does angle his head so that he blocks the sun shining in my eyes. And his hands are very gentle. "Do you want me to text Rob?"

I have no idea who Rob is. The driver, I guess.

"No."

I don't want to leave this spot. It's silly to think there is something special about this square foot of sand. Michael can come to me wherever he wants to. But it still feels special, holy. It slowly sinks in that Gavin is mixed up in this whole mess. . . . No. I don't want him to text anyone. Michael said it comes back to the one who was wronged, and suddenly I'm certain Gavin is who he meant. The sinking feeling in my stomach tells me that I'm not a big enough person to be happy that I get to fix him. Gavin is apparently as deeply embroiled in this mess as Natasha and I are. Which means it isn't a horrible coincidence that we are in the same class again. It's part of a divine plan.

I'm in so much trouble.

"Look, I don't know what you're trying to pull here," he says after a long moment. "But you're either high or seriously ill. Nobody collapses on the beach in the middle of the day and then is so fricking hard to rouse. You might as well tell me what's doing."

"No, no." I shake my head. "It's not like that."

"And why are you soaking wet?"

That I can answer. "I went swimming." And then I add smugly, "With dolphins."

"Now I know you're high."

"I even touched one!" I shove at his chest a bit. He doesn't

125

budge. Slowly he reaches for my wrist, his fingers easily encircling it. My heart gives a ridiculous leap at the touch of his hand on mine—until he tugs on my wrist. He's strong enough to pull my arm away but he's asking permission. I mutter under my breath as I unfold both arms so that he can see my clean, unmarred blue veins.

"I don't do drugs," I tell him. "You *know* that." But of course, he doesn't. How could he know anything about me? I look away, depressed and confused, and shift out of his arms.

He takes a deep breath and then turns so that he's sitting next to me, his long legs bent, his arms casually draped around them. "I don't want to see you hurt," he says.

I have to muffle my snort. Why in the world would he care about me, a little nerd from his senior year?

"If someone gave you something . . . you don't have to tell me who it was, but believe me, it's not a road you want to walk down. I saw a lot of smart people ruin their lives that way."

He must mean juvie. I can't imagine spending a year and a half locked away. We have gangs in St. Pete. We have big, ugly crime committed by straight-up killers. He was locked in with them for eighteen months.

"I'm sorry," I say. *For you*, though I don't say that. "But I'm not on drugs."

Gavin looks away in frustration. He glares at me, like he's going to say something, but then he looks away again. He hasn't shaved this morning and there's a faint shadow around his jaw from the stubble.

"Leni," he finally says. "I don't blame you for not trusting me. But I hope you believe me when I say that I've seen a lot of messed-up shit and I'd hate to see you pulled in over your head."

I hug my legs. I really don't know why he's being so nice.

"Gavin, it's not the right time for this."

"Just listen, okay?" he says, raking his hand through his hair, leaving sand behind.

I stand up.

I suddenly remember Sofia's words. *Let them show you the view from their side of the story. Listen, don't judge.* Gavin rises to his feet too, and even though he's taller than me, he looks pale and frightened.

I remember what a horrible time it was for him. After the initial feeling of vindication, that I'd been right not to believe in that golden charisma that everyone else was falling for, my heart ached for him.

It started out as a kind of joke. Some buddies of his wanted to help a woman who didn't have citizenship papers. No citizenship, no work. So Gavin hacked into the Florida DMV and got her a Social Security number. She was hired. Good deed done. That probably could have been the end of it—they hadn't been caught. But after they saw how well their philanthropic project went, they came up with a scheme that was a bit more entrepreneurial. Go in, grab a few extra numbers, nothing anyone was using, and sell them to undocumented workers. They sold each number for fifty bucks. They convinced themselves that it wouldn't hurt anyone. It was the easiest money any of them had ever made. There were rumors going around school at the time that Gavin was up to something, but none of us knew the full story until the trial, when everything came out.

Gavin always liked to push his luck. He was our school's living legend. He'd wheedle an extension on a due date and charm even the strictest teachers. He'd skip class and go hang out with the school's safety officer. He once popped into band practice, picked up a pair of drumsticks and played with the band, on beat and on time, for the hour and never went back again. He hacked into the school's official blog and slipped in an anonymous editorial about the school board's decision to cancel day care for high school mothers, a piece that was later picked up by the *Miami Herald*. Somebody at school once said his dad was some movie star in the eighties and I believe it. His dad wasn't around, so there was no way to know if this was just a rumor, but there was undeniably something about Gavin that was charismatic and magnetic, and I could totally picture his mom falling for a guy who looked like him. When he laughed, you couldn't help it, you had to turn to look.

Everyone let Gavin get away with his antics because he was brilliant, and we all knew he'd turn into something amazing. I guess he got used to living in a universe that played by his rules.

Until he was caught.

It received a lot of media attention; a high schooler hacking into the Florida DMV. One newspaper article said Pinellas County had just sent its smartest adolescent to jail. Depending on who was arguing in front of the judge, Gavin was either a prankster folk hero or the personification of everything wrong with the youth of today. All of us at Citrus Park High were riveted by the trial.

With the lingering presence of Michael still hanging over me, I fight the feeling that I'm responsible for what happens next. In my mind, Gavin's been someone to stay away from for a long time now. It's hard to redefine him as something else. Something more complicated.

Both of us turn to face the hypnotic repetition of waves on the shore. The waves in the Gulf are so gentle and sweet, only a few inches tall at their crest. I struggle against the feeling that Gavin's some sort of victim. But it saddens me to think about the blazing potential for greatness that we all saw in him in high school and how no one else will ever see him that way. People hear that he was in juvie and from then on, if he steps out of line, it reaffirms their belief that he's untrustworthy. I suddenly realize why he didn't fight the bogus cheating charges. He didn't think he would beat them. So what if this time he didn't do it. Who would believe him?

"Juvie wasn't all bad," he says quietly as if reading my mind.

"No?"

"I'm not saying I recommend it," he says wryly. His hands are shoved in his pockets, feet braced wide. He meets my sideways glance with an ironic one of his own. He's always looked older than his age. At seventeen he easily passed for twenty-one. Now that he's filled out more, he looks like a man in his midtwenties. That must have helped him. Big guys, tough guys, they command respect everywhere. He was a middle-class kid who maybe had a shoving match in junior high, up against guys who'd been fighting their whole lives; he needed all the advantages he could get.

It's wicked hot under the baking sun. A slight breeze gusts

up every so often, but with the sun glinting off the water and the pale sand, we're getting pummeled by heat from all directions. Sweat beads and pours freely down our faces and backs. I imagine the toxins of our past bleeding out with each drop.

"Judge Dillard was old-school," he says about the one adult who wasn't susceptible to his charms. He must sense my gaping disbelief at the fondness in his voice. "She was tough but fair." He shrugs. "She wanted to see what you were made of. If she believed in you, she wanted reports. You had to earn her respect, but once you did, she'd fight for you." Everyone in juvie had to attend classes, working toward a GED, and one of the teachers who volunteered there, Mr. Sninski, quickly took measure of Gavin's unusual abilities. Within a few weeks, he had Gavin teaching computer skills to the other teens.

"Everyone wants to be a hacker, so that helped a lot," Gavin says. "Plus a wicked right hook."

"Were there a lot of fights?"

"I wouldn't be a door warrior, so I put my boots on."

I blink at the slang.

"No one respects a britney," he explains, misinterpreting my blank stare.

"Britney?"

He coughs. "That's, uh, a disrespectful term for a coward."

"Door warrior?"

He laughs a bit at my tone.

"The guys who act tough as long as their cell door is locked but are little mice when the doors are open."

I wince at "cell door."

"Boots on?" But I already know the answer.

"Getting ready for a fight. It's like high school," he explains. "Only more brutal."

With the help of Mr. Sninski and Judge Dillard, Gavin won a scholarship to Tech, a full ride for four years. It made him believe in that old platitude that everything happens for a reason.

"Why Tech?" I always wondered if he wanted to leave Florida after his troubles. To leave us all behind.

"There was a professor at Tech, Tovar Isakson. He was like a freaking hero to me. He was the first to do some really groundbreaking research into algae as a fuel source. I wanted to learn everything there was to learn about that."

To hear Gavin tell it, it sounds like a fairy tale, an academic Cinderella story, except thanks to my snooping I know that it doesn't end with happily ever after. Even in his confessional mode, Gavin doesn't talk about what happened next or why he left school. He only says, with a grimace, that it didn't work out.

"The professor left school around the same time, anyway," he says. "Working on a start-up. I guess I should have stayed in Florida and hacked the lottery." He glances over and smiles wryly.

I blanch at how close to the truth his teasing is.

"I don't recommend it." I feel a sudden need to continue the spirit of confession. "We've spent it all, you know."

"That's rough."

I huff in a mirthless laugh. "My dad never worried about saving money. Even before we won the lottery, he spent more than we could afford. My parents had so many fights on the twenty-eighth of the month, it was a running joke."

My dad, part leprechaun, with that confident, mischievous

twinkle in his eyes. He doesn't look like that anymore. He was the one who bought the plot to build the house we live in, surprising my mom with it one day at dinner. The house that never felt like a home, because who calls a ten-thousand-square-foot Italianate monstrosity with six bedrooms, nine bathrooms, an indoor racquetball court, a dock with a boat lift, and a saltwater pool their home? Then again, maybe he was entitled to all that mad spending. Maybe it was better for this crazy, tainted money to leave our family quickly, extravagantly. He was the one who bought the ticket, after all. Maybe something about it bothered him.

"At least, before we won, he and my mom were working, so money was grounded in something real. He had to think, at least a little bit. Once money didn't have any kind of meaning, everyone went a little crazy. I don't know how else to explain it. We unmoored. Ticks can drink so much blood that they explode, you know? That's what we were like."

"That's harsh," he says. "You know, your parents helped pay for my defense team."

I blink at him in surprise. They never told me.

"Didn't do a very good job, did they?"

"At least my mom didn't have a mess of legal bills to deal with on top of everything else. I think that would have broken her completely."

I nod, accepting the thanks. My parents knew we went to school together—maybe that was enough for them to feel some sort of responsibility.

"There's no money left," I say. "Except for the trust fund

that they set up for me when I was ten. And everyone can't wait to get their hands on it."

I sense Gavin's surprise.

"It's a cliché, actually. Eighty percent of all lottery winners file for bankruptcy within ten years; we're just a few years ahead of schedule."

"But the trust fund is yours, right?" he says. "Nobody else has any right to it."

"No . . ."

"It is *your* money," he says.

"It's my parents' money. They parked it in a trust fund for seven years and now they need it. When the phone rings, nine times out of ten it's a creditor calling. There have been days when the water's been shut off and we flushed toilets with buckets of water from the pool. Which hasn't been swimmable in over a year, if you were wondering."

When I step away and walk to the surf, the warm water laps at my feet. Gavin follows. I haven't told any of my friends. I never pictured telling my big family secret to Gavin of all people.

"But nothing's going to change," Gavin argues, his quicksilver brain catching on to all the arguments I've tried to avoid for the past month. "They'll blow through your money and be back where they started in a couple of years, tops." I can't bear to look at him, so I watch a school of tiny fish dart by my feet, here and gone with desperate speed at the shift of the waves. I try not to think about the medi-spa calling. "Everyone had their chance to spend their money, and now you have yours."

His voice seeps into my unwilling ears. "Think about the difference you could make. At the right time, in the right place . . ." He shakes his head at the enormity of it, searches for the right words. "Leni, it could work a miracle."

It doesn't bear thinking about. My family needs that money. At the same time, we aren't entitled to it. What am I going to do?

"Leni, people get these game-changing moments once, maybe twice, their whole lives. I definitely blew mine. I picked the wrong door and"—he shrugs—"you saw what happened. I'm not trying to compare breaking the law to giving up your trust fund, but in some ways it's similar because you can never take it back."

I don't have an answer to give him.

Eventually we collect the trash that spilled out of my bag and brush the sand off our bottoms and our legs. Gavin insists I drink more water. I catch a long, speculative glance from him, but at least he's stopped insisting I tell him the name of my dealer.

I have the surprisingly warm and fuzzy feeling that if I gave him a name—if I had a name to give him—Gavin would be ready to step in and help me get clean.

Long after everyone boards on the van to head back to St. Petersburg, all sweaty and sunburned and pleased with their good works, I keep thinking about what Gavin said. With a million dollars, I could make a difference . . . and there is still Michael's mandate to consider. Gavin's odd choice of words resonates. *At the right time, in the right place . . . it could work a miracle.* God knows, I would love to make a miracle. It's just hard to believe that everything I need to make that happen is deposited at Regions Bank four blocks down the road from my house.

I have six days until my birthday.

It had been a long, hot and, let's be honest here, miserable morning. She was grimy and sweaty and she hated the fact that she could smell herself. Her third favorite shirt, a classic Lucky Charms from the eighties, was totally disgusting now, with large, unattractive sweat circles under the arms and across the back. She squirmed self-consciously and thought longingly of the cool shower waiting for her once they finally made it back, and the pile of neatly folded, clean-smelling shirts she would pick from. Beach cleanup had seemed like such a fun, noble thing to volunteer for. The sort of thing young, idealistic students were supposed to do. But it was such misery. Even though she'd slathered so much SPF 50 it felt like a layer of Vaseline on her skin, she'd managed to get sunburned and her neck and ears pulsed with heat in the cool van. Which meant she had tomato-red skin to look forward to for the next few days and she'd be that much more wrinkled in twenty years. Lovely. The beach had been depressingly trashed and even though they'd spent all morning picking up crap, it was obvious there was still more to do. The one cute guy who'd come along had sat way back on the ride over and then disappeared as soon as they'd arrived. And now, now he was cuddling with that freaking high school girl. To think she'd felt sorry for that awkward girl, and had tried to be friends. She harrumphed now in self-derision. The girl needed friends like a cactus needed thorns.

Joanie turned her back on the two of them. She rested her head on the cool glass and wondered what she was doing here. Her sister had majored in fashion design and now she was a buyer for J. C. Penney. But Joanie had already changed majors twice and she was twenty-one, not some teenager who could afford flitting from one thing to another. Even though the van was full of students, even though she'd been friendly and chatting with people all day, she felt utterly alone. Her stepdad had said they'd only pay for one more semester and then they were done, the last installment on a bad investment. What if she never figured things out? What if she was never anything but this lost underachiever trying to figure out what she wanted? Joanie snuck a glance at the high school girl again, feeling envy burning in her gut. That girl had it so easy. She was young and skinny and smart and had the cutest guy in class interested in her.

Life was so unfair.

Chapter Fourteen

I return home around lunchtime to an empty house. My note's gone from the counter, which means my mom read it and tossed it. There's no corresponding note from her saying where they are. I roll my eyes at the double standard. After a quick shower and a change of clothes, it's time to put my research experience to good use. Gavin's prophetic-like pronouncement only reinforces my feeling that everything is coming together and will be finished, one way or another, when the money's released.

I spend most of the afternoon online, following hunches, tracking down clues, until my eyes water and my wrists are sore, but after four straight hours I have nothing useful to show for it. I write down everything that Michael said, word for word when I can remember it, the general gist when I can't. It's disheartening to see such a short paragraph from such an earth-shattering visit. Have I already forgotten that much? Did he say so little? My brain cells rush in a frenzy, turning over every little memory stone, flipping through every memory folder, but there isn't much there.

The one who was wronged will come to you.

I could argue there are several possibilities for who that might be, but that's being disingenuous. Sticky strands of past hurts and bad choices cling to me and my family like kudzu vines, threatening to overtake us. The past is never dead, William Faulkner once wrote. It's not even past. I wonder about the ghosts he wrestled with.

I grab my bike and leave the sound of hyper sports broadcasters yapping in the nearly empty house. It's like a preheated oven outside and I slap at a slight sting on my arm and grimace at the smear of blood. Another dead mosquito. I hurriedly push off, knowing the breeze and speed of the bike will keep them away from me. It doesn't take much thought to push my pedaling feet in the direction of Natasha's tea shop.

It's a beautiful Florida afternoon, with Florida "mountains": those marshmallow cumulonimbus clouds that stretch thousands of feet in the air, floating impossibly huge and white against a cerulean sky. Other states have the Blue Ridge, the Smokies, the Rockies, but our cloud-mountain ranges re-form nearly every afternoon and give the landscape the same sense of depth.

The little silver bell above the door rings, announcing my arrival, though I half expect Natasha to have snuck out the back as I locked my bike. The ending scene from *It's a Wonder-*

ful Life flashes through my mind, the one when Zuzu Bailey says, "Look, Daddy. Teacher says, every time a bell rings an angel gets his wings." *Ha*, I think, *not my angel. He'd rip that bell off and crunch it between his diamond-hard teeth.*

Tibetan flutes play on the sound system. Two customers drink bubble tea and play Scrabble. To my pleasant surprise, Natasha's at the counter, frowning over her ledger. A typical Saturday afternoon scene. Except that Natasha's pale skin has a greasy, gray sheen. Her hair is lanky and unstyled. She wears her trademark backless dress, but it doesn't sit right on her. The bones in her shoulders jut like twigs.

I rest my elbows on the counter, waiting for her to look up, to smile her automatic welcoming-customer smile. She doesn't.

"Natasha?"

A frown crosses her face and she reluctantly glances up at me.

If Eddie has been living in a fog for the past few years, then Natasha's moved into a worse climate, like a category five hurricane. Her face is haggard, with deep, bruiselike bags under her eyes. The weight she's lost in the past few days seems like it all came from her face and chest.

"Natasha?" I ask gently.

"What?" she says, surly and annoyed.

Asking if everything is okay would be ridiculous. Asking what's wrong won't be much better. Her gaze returns to the ledger, so I decide to stick with that.

"Why are you going through your books? Is something wrong?"

She relaxes a fraction, though her brow remains furrowed.

"I keep going over the past few weeks and nothing adds up right." Exhaustion and frustration are plain in her voice. "Oh, screw it," she says, pushing the ledger away. "I can't deal with this today." Natasha not dealing with a problem in the shop? And then, reminding me that some things never change, she turns her bloodshot green eyes on me. "Why are you here, anyway?"

"I wanted to make sure you were okay."

"Please." She rolls her eyes.

"We need to talk."

"I don't have the time to put up with this crap," she says loudly. The two customers playing Scrabble suddenly grow very quiet. "I've got a million things to do, Lenore, okay?" I stiffen as she spits out my full name. "There're, like, fifty invoices to go through, I have six bills that are overdue, two customers have complained about spoiled milk in their tea and, if you can believe it, there's a health inspection coming any day. I told you all there is to tell you. I'm not going to say anything else, so just drop it, okay?"

The shop is dead silent except for those damn flutes. Someone clears their throat nervously and chairs scrape back as the two customers quickly leave the shop.

She glares at me, haggard and defiant, even as her eyes grow translucent with tears. Then she whirls with all the style and verve that I expect from her and pushes through the beaded curtain, slamming her office door for good measure.

The flutes finally finish and in their place, a sad, haunting ukulele comes on in the now deserted tea shop.

When a customer walks in, I do the right thing and move

behind the counter to serve her, and the next few customers that come in. I work the register and make drinks, the numb shock gradually fading. The lack of sleep, the stress and the guilt over what I'm planning sit uneasily. I didn't realize how much I was counting on my sister to help me through this.

Natasha finally emerges from the office, old smeared makeup scrubbed off. A new, poorly applied coat of lipstick and dark eyeliner bring her face back to something resembling normal, though it's an impostor taking a turn at playing Natasha. She's dull and slow as she steps up to the counter and opens her ledger again without ever looking at me. She doesn't thank me or in any way recognize that I did her a favor; she won't acknowledge, not even with a facial expression or body language, what passed between us two nights ago.

I finally realize, truly and fully, that Natasha will not help me solve this problem. The whole family depends on me, possibly our very souls depend on me, and in the end, they're all going to hate me for it.

"This is your mess I'm cleaning up," I say, slamming down a dirty mug. "You don't want to hear this? Fine. Don't." I rip off my apron and throw it on the floor. We're alone in the shop and I don't hold anything back. "Don't listen to the fact that I had an angel visit me. Twice! Or that I have to figure out how to undo this curse you brought on the family. Don't help me figure it out. Fine. You say you did something evil because the devil made you? That you didn't have a choice? Natasha, all you've done your whole life is make choices that fit what you want and what you need. No one made you do this. No one!"

Taking a lovely page out of Natasha's own book, I stomp off, ignoring her calling out to me. The front door doesn't slam, but it still feels good to hear her cries of "Leni! Leni! Come back!" silenced as the door closes.

My heart is racing and my hands on the handlebars feel a little trembly, the aftermath of an adrenaline rush. Surely, Michael is gnashing his teeth at my behavior. If he has teeth. But I don't regret it. I'm on my own with this. It's better to face that.

"Make Emmett love me," she had said, her heart racing. By asking him to do this for her, she was taking an irrevocable step. He knew everything about her by then, even her thoughts. It was more intimate than sex. She knew she couldn't trust him, yet she felt this deep connection, this terrible weakness around him. He was charming and dangerous and she was so desperately turned on and terrified at the same time that she couldn't think straight. Emmett was her only anchor. As long as he stayed, everything would be okay.

"I can't make him love you, baby girl. I can't even make him stay," he said, rolling his shoulders in tight frustration. "That whole free-will bullshit. I can't make anyone do anything." Some of the magnetism she'd fallen for splintered under his pissed-off admission, and that scary abyss she sensed about him flickered between the cracks.

She could taste the ashy disappointment, Emmett slipping away. Everything lost. But she was smart enough to keep her mouth shut and wait for the rest of it.

"Now, luck—good or bad—I can help you with that," he said, his grin back in place. "I can make good cars break down, I can distract drivers. I can make a roof leak or a house catch fire." He

raised a questioning eyebrow. She quickly shook her head no. "I can lead you to buried treasure." He laughed at her expression. "There's sunken treasure right here in Florida, baby girl, all those Spanish galleons with looted Incan gold. Then again, you've got the body of a rock star, I can give you the voice to go with it. It'd be a piece of cake to hook you up with a music exec and land you a contract, baby girl." He licked his lips as he leered at her. An uncomfortable hot flush crept under her skin as her heart kicked up in fear and excitement. He was toying with her. She had to fight to keep from crossing her arms protectively over her chest. She didn't say anything, just looked away. "I can make you win the lottery."

Natasha froze.

"Ah," he drawled. "Finally heard something you're interested in?" He leaned in until that tricky, mesmerizing mouth was right next to her, his breath tickling her skin. "It'd be a smart move, baby girl. Money makes everything better." She shivered as his lips brushed oh so softly against her ear. "Money fixes everything."

They negotiated, right there on the spot. Powerball was at seventy million—if her family took the lump payment, after taxes they'd keep twenty-two. All she had to do was get her dad to buy a ticket tonight. The drawing was tomorrow.

"I expect a little something for my trouble," he said casually. "A favor."

Thinking frantically about what that might mean, she insisted that it couldn't involve hurting family or anyone she knew. She was proud of herself for thinking of that, because around him, his charm and that crackling energy, it was hard to think of anything bad happening at all.

A part of her knew she should wait, she should sleep on it. Think about loopholes or the fine print or what it could all mean. But the thing was, she didn't want to think. Emmett was leaving her, leaving Florida forever. If she won, maybe he would stay, because it would be so much fun to be millionaires together. In the tiny quiet part of her heart that told her Emmett wasn't leaving because of money, and money wouldn't keep him, she also thought that if Emmett left, maybe it wouldn't hurt as much if she turned the family rich. They would all love her and be so grateful to her, it would all be worth it anyway.

So they agreed. When she went home that night, she lay in bed wondering if it was all a big lie and he was having fun at her expense. Right before she fell asleep, she'd almost convinced herself that nothing special would happen tomorrow.

She watches as her sister leaves the tea shop, righteous indignation in her every step. The girl angels come to. Natasha shudders.

"You're better off without my help, Leni," she whispers. "I ruin everything I touch."

Chapter Fifteen

It's nearly dark outside by the time I'm home, but there are lights glowing in the windows, making the house look alive. Smooth jazz pours from the built-in speakers in the foyer. My parents haven't played music through the housewide sound system in ages and I've long grown used to entering a house that's dark except for the flickering blue light of the big screen TV down the hall.

There's no dinner under way in the kitchen and my brother isn't parked in the recliner.

"Hello?" I call out.

"Hi!" my mom trills from their bedroom.

I enter a transformed suite. Their king-size bed has a new bright red comforter with a white coral design and a small mountain of pillows. The tracks on the carpet from a recent cleaning are still there and there's a fresh smell of lemon polish. It's the best their room has looked in months.

My mom pops out of her bathroom as I enter their room.

"Wow," I say.

Her hair is glossy, in a short, stylish bob with soft, tasteful highlights. She's put on full makeup, but in new, softer shades, and she's wearing a beautiful periwinkle pantsuit that brings out her new tan.

She grins at my reaction.

"Mom, you look awesome." I feel like a traitor mentally adding up how much all this improvement costs. Haircut and color, new makeup, new outfit, tanning and—if I'm not mistaken—new pearl earrings.

"We haven't been out in ages," my mom says happily. "I can't believe how long it's been since I've updated my colors."

"Where are you guys going?"

"It's a small event, heavy hors d'oeuvres, but you know, we've been so cooped up lately, we decided to have fun with it."

"What's it for?"

"Angel investors informational meeting," she says.

"Angel investors," as I've found out over the years, is a lovely term for people with money who are willing to throw it at various start-ups, with the hopes that one of them will strike it big. We've lost millions that way. My mom mentions it casually, as if it's of no significance, as if this invitation isn't someone salivating over the rumor that they're going to be flush again.

They used to get invited to a lot of these events. They always enjoyed getting wined and dined, the fawning attention from eager businessmen. I didn't really notice when these invitations stopped coming, but it's definitely been a couple of years. Is this invitation a sign that news has leaked that my trust fund is maturing, or is this fund-raiser using an old list for potential investors?

"What does an entrepreneur want with you?"

My mother smiles and shrugs, as if to say, *Who cares, it's a party!* In the face of her great excitement, I suddenly realize that my parents haven't been invited to any kind of social gathering in over a year. Not one. My heart twists at the thought.

My father comes out of his bathroom, mopping his face to get rid of a few traces of shaving cream. His crisp white button-down shirt is half-unbuttoned and my mom tsks at him to hurry up. He pulls a suit jacket from the closet, the price tag still hanging from the sleeve.

"Dad?" I raise an eyebrow.

"They sent us an invitation weeks ago, but we just decided to go. The more I read about it, the more interesting it sounds." It's the same excited, optimistic tone that has preceded so many bad investments. "Renewable energy. That's the future right there. And getting in on the ground level, that's where the big money is."

In the past, I tuned him out when he got to this point. The lure of "big" money has proven false every time. But this time it's *my* money we're talking about, so I keep listening as my father launches into a recitation of the company's bullet points.

"Our country runs a tremendous trade deficit in oil every

day. There's an environmental effect to burning oil. There's an economic factor. But what's the alternative? Solar and wind power are hard to store and transport." It's great that he's fired up about environmentally responsible fuel alternatives, but this isn't new information. Anyone selling it as something groundbreaking is a complete con artist.

My mother picks out a tie for him and he struggles to tie it in front of their large full-length mirror. I'm at the edge of their bed, torn between affection and exasperation.

"So what's the solution?"

"I'm getting to it. The man who runs this company discovered algae that produce fuel. Can you imagine it? From garbage! It's fantastic! They can even grow in brackish water." He starts gesturing with his hands and the tie tying falls apart. My mom steps in to finish the job. "He's sitting on the future of energy."

"You don't think it sounds too good to be true?"

Some of what I feel leaches out in my tone. My mother gives me a warning look, but it takes a lot more than that to dampen my dad's enthusiasm once it sparks.

"I'm sure he's simplifying things in his prospectus. He knows his investors aren't scientists. But his overall premise isn't overstating the potential—in fact, he's selling it short. Honey, this man was a college professor and he left his job to make this happen. This isn't a scam."

"Wait. He was a professor?" It's the second time today I've heard about a brilliant professor who left his job to try to make an idea come to life.

My dad, sensing a chink in my skeptical armor, grins.

"Sure was, a professor at Tech. His name is Isakson. Tovar Isakson."

My skin prickles with sudden cold. It's the same person Gavin tried to study with at Tech. Maybe it's because I encountered an angel today, maybe it's because I know winning the lottery was a setup, but I'm suddenly convinced that it wasn't an accident Gavin was kicked out of school. It wasn't a prank gone wrong or a random hater. There had to be some unnatural influence at work. That's why Michael came. Because something malicious and bad interfered to get Gavin kicked out of Tech. Since we "owe," karmically speaking, Michael tasked me to fix it. Getting Gavin back in contact with the one person he wanted to spend time with at Tech is a fantastic start at fixing a huge problem.

"Can I come with you?" I ask.

My parents exchange a wide-eyed look of surprise.

"Sure, sweetheart," my dad says.

"Of course, sweetie," my mom echoes. She eyes my shorts and T-shirt. "But we need to find you something to wear."

I know what I have to do. Gavin's face on the beach this morning, Michael's voice exhorting me to fix it, Natasha's charismatic charmer—all swirl before me, and for the first time since Wednesday, I have the beginnings of a plan.

"And, um, can I invite a friend to come with me?"

My mom's eyes nearly pop out with delighted surprise.

"Yes." I dryly answer her unasked question. "It's a boy."

She squeals like a young girl. "You have a boyfriend?"

"Mom!" I flush bright red at the thought of her calling Gavin that.

She looks ready to burst with curiosity. It's with visible effort that she holds back her questions.

"You've heard of him," I admit. This is going to be interesting. "Gavin Armand's back in town."

"The kid who went to jail for hacking? That's who you're dating?"

"No, Dad," I say. "It's not like that." They both face me, waiting for an explanation. "First of all, we are friends, not dating. Second, I think that he is trying to be a better person." And we're not even really friends, more like . . . allies. Michael must believe there's more to him than meets the eye, but somehow I don't see that working as a compelling argument. "Let me text him, okay? See if he can even make it."

"He's an actual juvenile delinquent." My dad sits on the bed, shaking his head, lost for words. "This is every parent's nightmare!"

"Peter," my mom says. "Let her be."

"We're in the same SHCC class," I say, swallowing with difficulty. "This will be great for a project we're working on for the professor. You know, she mentioned in her lecture about the dangers of carbon in the oceans and how clean energy needs to be a huge priority—"

"You're in the same SHCC class?" my mom interrupts. "You didn't tell me that."

She and my dad exchange the our-teenager-is-keeping-things-from-us look.

I probably should have told her before this, especially now that Gavin told me they paid for his defense. My mom always likes to know who is in class with me, who I spend time with. In fact, it is really unusual that she hasn't already grilled me on what SHCC is like.

"He told me you guys paid for his defense," I say, moving the conversation along. "Why did you?"

"He was your friend," my mom says, simply.

"We barely knew each other," I protest. "He was in one of my classes, that's it."

"He went to your school and I knew his mom from PTA. It broke my heart to see what she was going through."

"That was a truly kind thing to do," I say. "Gavin told me how much it meant to them, especially his mom."

My parents exchange a soft look and a small smile, nicely distracted. I forget how incredible my parents are sometimes.

"One look at his poor mother, and Dad and I knew we had to do something. No one wants to see their child pay so dearly for a mistake he made in high school."

Too bad no one was looking out for Natasha back then.

"But that doesn't mean it's okay to hang out with a convicted criminal," my dad adds, heading to the bathroom.

Knowing what happened at Tech, I'm pretty sure Gavin wouldn't want to see his old professor again, so I don't mention Isakson will be there, only that it's a fund-raiser for a company he might be interested in, which is technically true. After Gavin texts back yes, my dad grumbles some more under his breath about character and a lack of trust, even as my mother elbows him sharply. As soon as she knows we're both joining them tonight, she gets in an absolute tizzy about what I should wear. Clothes aren't something I usually think too much about but her excitement is contagious. My stomach does a funny little flip at the thought of seeing Gavin tonight, helping him connect with his old professor. It feels right, the way events are falling into place.

My mom and I hurry to my room, only to stare disappointedly in my closet.

"Oh, Leni," my mom says. "This looks like an orphan's closet. Don't you care about how you look at all?" Jeans, khakis, a couple of knee-length skirts and some out-of-date dresses hang crookedly on metal hangers. I wore one dress to my uncle's funeral. There's the dress I wore to Steeped's opening, but it looks like something a thirteen-year-old would wear, probably because I was thirteen the last time I wore it.

"I care," I say, stung. "But how often do I need a cocktail dress? Never."

My mother mutters something about whether we can make it to Nordstrom's and be back in time for the party. All of a sudden, her face lights up.

"Come on," she says, and drags me down the hall.

We go to the closet in Natasha's old room and sure enough, there are dozens of dresses hanging there, long forgotten. Flipping through them with the crisp, professional motions of a veteran shopper, my mom selects three dresses. I make a face. Natasha and I have never worn the same size and besides, her taste in clothes is not what I like.

"Trust me," my mom says. So I strip and step into a silky, beaded red shift. My mom zips up the back and I shimmy to get the dress in place. I can't remember the last time I wore anything but shorts or jeans and an old T-shirt. Natasha's room has a large full-length mirror in one corner. I walk over to it barefoot, toes gripping the beige carpet, and barely recognize myself in the reflection. Red is a bold color, not for blending in. Which of course appeals to Natasha but I'm shocked that it looks good on me. Natasha picked indigo for her room when the house was decorated, and against the dark inky-purple walls, the red dress glows like a jewel.

"I like it," I say.

My mom eyes me critically, rising from her perch on the edge of the peacock-patterned satin quilt on the bed and examining the dress from different angles.

"It's not bad," she says, rather noncommittally. "But let's try the other ones."

Next is a long, tailored sleeveless dress in apple green. Again, it's nothing I would ever have picked out for myself but it looks amazing against my tan and brings out the green in my eyes.

"I like this one even better," I say. And for the first time in a long time, I turn to her and ask, "What do you think?"

"Let's see how the last one looks on you," my mom says. I finally understand why shopping can be so much fun. I'm actually excited to try it on. She unzips the dress and I step out. Wearing only underwear and a bra, I lean over and kiss her. She grins at me and then kisses me on the cheek.

The last dress she picked is pale lavender, the exact shade of the sky when the sun dips below the horizon. It's made from crushed velvet and stops an inch above my knees. My favorite part is a narrow sash embroidered with shells that ties under my breasts. The dress still has the price tag on it.

My mom zips up the back and ties the sash. I step in front of the mirror, surprised by the slender, lovely young woman staring back at me. My arms look golden and strong, my legs look long and lean. In this dress, I have breasts. In this dress, I am beautiful.

"This one," I say.

My mom straightens the straps so that they cover my bra, eyes me critically and then smiles.

"We've got a winner," she says. "Now let's do something with your hair."

Chapter Sixteen

Despite the trendy address off Beach Boulevard, the fund-raiser is at a modest little Chinese restaurant, a place I must have passed dozens of times and never noticed; not the usual chic spot these things tend to take place in. There's a small, handwritten sign on the front door announcing the place is closed for a private party. My mom exchanges a mewl of disappointment with my dad before they gamely enter the room.

A small buffet holds several covered dishes warming over a flame. Two large platters of greasy egg rolls sit untouched. The tables and chairs from the restaurant have been optimistically pushed up against the walls to leave the middle clear for the mingling crowd but there are only a dozen people there, making the place look sad and abandoned. My parents and I are ridiculously overdressed. A few of the people in the room are in jeans; two wear shorts. People eye us, probably wondering when we're going to realize we're at the wrong event.

The muscles in my shoulders tense in embarrassment. Now I know why my parents were invited. The professor used an old who's-who list.

A short man with a tidy, close-trimmed beard and a jacket with leather patches on the elbows, incongruous in the Florida heat, hurries to us.

"Welcome," he says. "I'm glad you could make it tonight. I'm Tovar Isakson, the CEO, director, founder, and jack-of-all-trades for AlgaeGo."

I make a face at the company name. It sounds like some pharmaceutical answer to an obscure skin disease.

"Peter Kohn," my dad says, unfazed and extending a hand. Looking at the two of them, my dad hale and buff in a crisp button-down shirt with a gleaming designer tie, shaking hands with the slim and shabby Isakson, you'd be hard-pressed to guess who was the CEO of a company with groundbreaking technology and who was the man about to lose his house to foreclosure. "This is my wife, Linda," my dad continues. My mom's game face is back on and she shakes Isakson's hand with a warm smile. Another perfect example of poise and confidence. "And our beautiful daughter, Lenore."

"Leni," I correct.

The professor shakes my hand firmly before turning his attention to my parents. "Let me take you to the back. I'm about to start my presentation."

My mom looks beseechingly at me, less than happy at the prospect of being lectured to, but I shake my head to let her know I'm staying by the door to wait for Gavin.

With so few people in the restaurant, it's easy to spot Gavin when he arrives. I can't stop that glad little leap of excitement at seeing him, my stomach in full butterfly mode. He's dressed up a bit for this too, wearing a pale-blue button-down and khaki slacks.

"Wow," he says when he sees me in Natasha's dress.

I feel a blush coming on. "This old thing," I say.

By now, the professor has darkened the room for his presentation and from the look of the screen over Gavin's shoulder, it includes PowerPoint slides. My poor mother.

"Looks like class is starting."

Gavin turns to the back of the restaurant. I know the exact moment when he recognizes the man at the lectern. He freezes and then pales.

"I have to go," he says.

"Gavin," I say softly. "Stay."

"You don't understand, I *can't*."

"Come on," I wheedle. "You're already here. Stay."

"That's Professor Isakson," he says, almost desperately, edging back toward the door. "That man hates me." He suddenly turns those razor eyes on me. "You did this on purpose."

"You should hear what he has to say," I say, not denying it. "And maybe he'll listen to you too."

He presses his lips in a tight white line.

"What have you got to lose?" I coax.

"My self-respect?" He's only half-joking.

"Please," I scoff. "Like you ever had any." I offer him my hand. He clasps it in the same instinctive motion. There's tension vibrating in his arm and I squeeze his hand.

"This is your revenge because I said you do drugs, isn't it?"

"Just listen to him, okay?"

"Why not." He flashes his cocky grin. "No problem."

I get the sense that he only agreed because he's not a britney and that he's putting his boots on.

We're the last ones to sit and, as soon as we do, Isakson starts.

Slide after slide—graphs, projections, equations—it's all there. The different algae strains, the possible food source, the fuel output, and the shining diamond of his plan: unlike ethanol, which needs prime farm land, these algae grow in brackish water that is otherwise unusable. The man has his ducks in a row.

When the professor finishes his presentation, the lights come back on and there's a smattering of applause. Unfortunately, from the slack, uninterested faces of the half dozen people making up his audience, it's clear that most of them are clueless. My mother, who fell asleep, wakes up with a start when the lights come on. My dad looks bored and distracted as he fiddles with his cell phone.

An anxious look crosses Isakson's face as he senses the mood of his crowd.

"Are there any questions?" he asks.

Awkward silence descends. No one makes eye contact with

the professor. One of the employees of the restaurant pushes in a metal trolley to gather used plates and the wheels make an annoying little chirp with every rotation. *Chirp, chirp, chirp.* Isakson waits for questions. There were too many chairs set up for his talk, which only highlights how few people came.

"When will the algae be up and operational?" someone asks.

"Excellent question." Isakson bobs his head nervously. "There are several promising strains that we will continue to test in the coming months. Once we isolate the best performer, we will begin negotiations for land."

"So you're, what, more than a year away from any kind of product launch?"

"We hope to move sooner than that," Isakson says vaguely, but everyone in the audience can hear the truth. He's nowhere close to being up and running.

He waits a beat.

"Any other questions?" he asks. The silence grows heavy and he turns to straighten a stack of handouts on the low table next to him. "I'd be happy to speak with any of you in private," he adds.

There's a sporadic attempt at applause.

"Come on," I say to Gavin. "Let's go talk to him."

"Bad idea, Kohn."

But I tug on his arm and he follows. People are still sitting, shaking off the stupefying effects of a thirty-minute PowerPoint presentation, and Gavin and I reach the professor before anyone else.

"Hi," I say.

Isakson looks grateful for someone to talk to but disappointed that it's a couple of teenagers. His brown-and-red beard has a lot of gray, but there is something youthful about him. He isn't much taller than me and I am in the unusual position of feeling somewhat protective of an adult who is decades my senior.

"Leni Kohn," I remind him. "My parents are Peter and Linda."

"Yes, yes, of course," he says effusively, pumping my hand.

"This is my friend, Gavin Armand."

The professor blinks at the mention of Gavin's name.

"Mr. Armand," he says, frowning, eyeing Gavin up and down. "I didn't expect to see you again. I believe I made my thoughts clear a year ago."

Gavin tenses next to me and his face goes white.

"Professor," I begin, horrified.

A man with a huge gut and the squinty eyes of an avid fisherman comes up to the professor. "Interesting concept you've got there," he says as he hitches up his pants in back. Isakson, with an ingratiating smile, turns to him.

"Excuse me, Professor," I say, but the grown-ups are talking and he all but pats my head in dismissal, unwilling to waste time on a couple of non–financially contributing, and therefore useless, teenagers.

My parents are mingling with a couple they know and Gavin has this awful, cold look on his face. There isn't anything here for me to do.

I interrupt my parents' social chitchat. "We're heading out," I announce. My mom eyes Gavin, seemingly absorbing every possible detail and clearly noting the frozen look on his face, but other than reaching out to shake hands with him and saying in a cool voice that it's been a while, she doesn't react.

"Gavin." My dad looks him over with a gimlet eye, a flush rising in his face.

"Hello, sir," Gavin says. He reaches out to shake hands and it is a long, insulting moment before my dad shakes his hand. "Thank you for letting me spend time with Leni."

My dad doesn't answer.

"Don't stay out too late," my mom says, her hand visibly tightening on my dad's arm like she's holding him back. "Keep your phone on in case we need to reach you."

I kiss her cheek.

"Love you too." She smiles. She kisses me back, then wipes at the lipstick stain on my cheek. "Be safe."

I nod. Their automatic mistrust is the cost Gavin pays for choosing the wrong door. What will it cost me if I choose the wrong one?

Gavin and I slip out the door.

With an inky-black night above and dark churning water below, we lean on the railing at the pier and watch the tiny lights of fishing boats out in the Gulf. The pier's a good twenty feet above the water, low enough for the fishermen's lines to reach the water, high enough to catch a nice breeze and a great view.

The wide expanse of water and the gulf air do little to clear the tension.

"It could have been worse," I finally say.

Gavin exhales loudly. A soft, salty breeze blows our way.

"I'm so screwed." His voice is grim in the dark. He tilts his head back, eyes closed, radiating defeat.

"Gavin—"

"I've been following his work. It could literally change the world." He pushes off the railing, kicks the post and shoves his hands in his pockets. "Penicillin. Movable-type printing press. The steam engine. He could make one of those moments happen except he's clueless. You saw him." In the weird orange light from the lamps, Gavin's eyes look like dark pits, his face like a skeleton.

"Yeah, but—"

"I can help him," he says, his voice almost shaking with passion. "This is what I've been working on. Isakson is a brilliant scientist, but he's not a businessman. He doesn't get it. You saw him tonight!"

The fund-raiser we left that wasn't going to raise any funds flashes through my mind.

"He thinks he needs to have the perfect formula, the optimal combination of algae and fuel, and once he has that, he thinks he needs to buy land to set up the tanks."

"That makes sense."

"No." Gavin shakes his head. "It's backward. People need to see something happening. They don't need perfect, they need progress. And it's ass-backward to buy the land. He needs to lease it. He needs to find cheap land that people aren't using—which should be a freaking piece of cake since he wants brackish water—and with little capital outlay, get some equipment and get started.

"After Hurricane Erica last year, tons of farmland in South Florida was flooded. Those fields are shot for the next three years. If he wanted, he could rent hundred of acres for peanuts. Why drop hundreds of thousands of dollars on a small piece of property when you don't even know that the company will be around in six months? And it won't be if he doesn't get moving."

"Wow." I think about it for a second. "That makes a lot more sense."

His smile is a pale cousin of his typical confident grin.

"It's not that amazing. But he needs to do it. He just doesn't know it. He's so focused on the science that he's missed the boat on the business of running a company."

We stare out at the water, the black wavelets lapping at the barnacle-encrusted pillars below us.

"How do you know all of this, anyway?"

"I met a lot of entrepreneurs at juvie."

"Really?"

"A drug dealer is like any small-business owner. They got inventory, they got customers, they got cash-flow problems and competition. It's no different from any other business in that sense. It sparked my interest—not in drug dealing, I mean, in business. I took some business classes at Tech and afterward, I studied on my own. I thought it would be cool to start my own company. Once I learned about Isakson's company, I started poking around commercial-property sites. They're out there if you look for them."

"So how come he remembers your name from Tech?" I ask hesitantly. "You weren't there very long."

"I was the last one to check out this book that later turned up missing the pages necessary for a tough assignment," he says flatly. "Someone accused me of doing it. Anonymously. Just try proving you don't have something in your possession." He shrugs. "It's impossible. I lost my scholarship, I was kicked out of school. And yeah, Professor Isakson remembers my name," he says dryly. "The assignment was for his class."

"That doesn't even make sense. Like people couldn't just read it online? What is this, 1870?"

He laughs hollowly. "Isakson's old-school. He gave us this big lecture at the start of the semester about libraries and books and how our generation is losing touch with what it means to research. Part of his class was about library skills. He made sure we had to use old, rare books that weren't online. Half the stuff you couldn't even take out of Special Collections. No scanners. No Xerox machines. These books were historic. He wanted us to read this thing. It wasn't a published book really—it was the student notebook of Francis William Aston."

I nod, fake-impressed by a name I don't recognize.

"Uh, he won the Nobel Prize for chemistry in the 1920s?"

"Oh, right. Cool."

"It was kind of incredible, actually. To hold the notes that this guy wrote when he was a student, it was unbelievable. The librarian had a fit that an entire class of underclassmen was going to be handling it. I had to wear gloves. Which made it even shittier that someone cut out some pages. They changed their policy after that: no undergrads could access Special Collections without a TA."

"Did you ever find out who accused you?"

He shakes his head.

"Isn't that unconstitutional or something?"

He laughs hollowly again. "I didn't go to jail, I was kicked out of school. I doubt a school's honor code falls under federal jurisdiction."

"It should." Gavin's story reinforces my belief that he was framed by an expert, the best of the best. What did Natasha's charmer promise his dupe at Tech? And how much is it biting him on the ass now?

Gavin puts his arm around me like a pal giving me a one-armed squeeze for my loyal support. I shiver at the sudden warmth of his arm. To mask it, I fiddle with my purse and pull out a pack of gum.

"Professor Isakson left school after that, you know," he says, accepting a piece of gum. "In his interview with the school paper, he said he was ready for a new opportunity but I always felt like it was my fault. Like, if it wasn't for me, he'd still be teaching." He's trying to be flippant, but it's obvious how much those words still hurt. It's that hurt that worms its way through my defenses.

"So we have to figure out how to get your business plan to the professor, convince him that you were framed and that you're not the embodiment of the self-entitled, lazy future of America." I blow a bubble and it pops loudly. "Easy."

Gavin laughs and hugs me to him. He was always easy with his hugs at school, always physical with everyone, like a big puppy. I don't take it personally.

"Sure," he agrees. "Easy as pie."

"It's your business plan that could do it," I say earnestly, pushing out of his arms. "You can't cheat your way into an idea like that. That company, what does he call it?"

"AlgaeGo."

"That's a stupid name," I say, "but whatever. AlgaeGo is his baby. Right now, it's failing. If you do something that gets his company really going, that lets people see how beautiful his baby really is, then he's going to love you. And since it's not something you can copy or steal, it'll prove what you're capable of. He'll be forced to reconsider."

"It's not that easy," Gavin says. "He doesn't even want to talk to me—why would he listen or believe anything I say?" Even though Gavin is arguing against me, there's a spark of excitement in his voice.

"Because you come with hard numbers," I say. "You track down the landowner of a flooded farm, you dazzle them with your charm, you negotiate a fantastic deal on behalf of AlgaeGo and then you present him with the figures. No one else knows enough about the company, or cares enough, to do it. Once you have the deal worked out, it'll speak for itself."

"Dazzle them with my charm?"

"Don't make me repeat it," I laugh. "The fact that you're

taking the time to pull this deal together is going to change everything for Isakson. I'm assuming the land will be cheap?"

"That's a safe assumption," he says with no false modesty. We share a grin.

"All teachers dream about the student that goes above and beyond the basic assignment," I argue. "Here, you're not only doing that, you're making an assignment where none existed. And you're only doing it for the success of his company. How could he not be impressed? How could he not reevaluate his opinion?"

"And what, I negotiate as AlgaeGo's agent? I don't have that authority."

"Gavin, seriously? You say you're the company's agent but that you have to present any final offer to the owner himself. It's not that hard."

He angles his head away from me, hiding his face. That amazing brain of his is firing, looking for holes in my argument, following my logic to its conclusion.

After a moment, he nods.

"Maybe you're right." He shrugs coolly. "At this point, there's not much I could do to lower his opinion."

"First thing to do when you're in a hole is to stop digging." I echo my dad's folksy truism. "Next is to figure out how to climb out."

"Is that so?" There's amusement in his voice and if nothing else, I've given him the needed nudge away from morose depression and toward constructive action.

Michael, I think as I glance up at the starry skies, *I hope this works for you.* I'm sure it's only atmospheric changes that make the brightest star in the evening sky look like it's winking at me.

We linger there at the edge of the pier, the briny air blowing possibilities and ideas our way.

In two hours, it will be five days until my birthday.

Chapter Seventeen

I skip school on Monday morning—a first for Goody Two-Shoes little me. As I ride my bike in the quiet downtown streets after rush hour, I half expect some responsible citizen to call in a truancy officer to haul me back to school.

The start-up office is located on the third floor of a nearly vacant office building, one of the older ones that manage to be both stately and dilapidated. It's on the unofficial border between the new, shiny high-rises, galleries and boutiques that stay empty all day, now that the economy has turned and no one wants to spend three hundred dollars on a strange-looking vase, and the part of the city that even during the boom years refused to spruce up and ditch its quick marts selling pressed Cuban sandwiches and cheap beer (ice cold!). Where weirdos loiter and the homeless, grungy and disgruntled sprawl on benches in the middle of the day. I lock my bike to a lamppost and hope it'll be there when I return. The heavy leaded-glass door to the building isn't locked.

The office suite has a stained, threadbare carpet, windows so smudged they barely let in light, and office furniture that looks like it was picked up off the curb on Big Trash Day. There's a main reception area with dusty fake plants, a framed poster of the company logo, and a big messy desk with no one sitting behind it. Of the two doors off the reception area, one is open to an empty room. Muffled sounds come from behind the closed door.

I walk over and knock loudly.

The muffled sounds cease immediately and after a short pause, the door opens. Isakson looks at me quizzically, apparently unable to place me.

"Yes?" he asks.

"I'm Leni Kohn," I say. "I'm here to help you."

He invites me into his office and I sit on a hard plastic chair, fighting nerves, trying to sound like a confident investor instead of a nervous teenager taking a huge gamble. Isakson wears a light blue collared shirt and pale, narrow jeans that somehow don't look American. There's a large carafe of French-press coffee sitting on the ledge of the dirty window, which strengthens my impression that he wasn't raised in the States. Europe or maybe the Middle East, though when he spoke on Saturday, he didn't have an accent, just a slightly different way of pronouncing some words, putting the emphasis on the wrong syllable.

I spent all of Sunday learning about business models and angel investors from Delaney Cramer, a businesswoman and family friend that my parents helped out a couple of years back. She was the one who helped them set up my trust fund in the first place. She's always been fond of me and several times has tried to talk me into studying finance when I go to college. We spent two hours on the phone while she gave me a crash course in successful start-up business models. Angel investors bridge the gap for a small company that has tapped funds from friends and family but is too small for venture capitalist firms to bother with. Because there's such a high risk that all their investment money will be lost if the young company doesn't make it—which I know very well from my parents' unfortunate investment experiences—angel investors usually require terms that give them a very high return on their investments. Which gave me an idea of how to pull this off.

"If you're looking for investors, you're wasting your time talking to my parents," I begin. "It's not their money. It's mine."

The professor's eyebrows rise as he looks at me like I'm a puppy claiming to be Napoleon. One office wall is lined with cheap bookcases bending under the weight of dozens of huge binders full of papers. Stacks of papers in various heights have been placed on the floor, like a child's model city. It's the office of a busy man who doesn't have time or money to waste. Sure enough, he lets me know it.

"Why would a young woman want to spend her money on a start-up that has a seventy-five percent chance of failure?"

I knew this question would come and I was prepared.

"Would you ask my parents that? Would you question any

other investor that wanted to join the company? Because if *that's* your strategy, you need to increase your chances of failure. Ninety-nine percent sounds more likely."

He looks stunned and a hurt look flashes in his eyes. Crap. Not the way to win him over.

"Believe me"—I grip the nubby fabric–covered armrests of the cheap office chair—"I may be younger than most of your investors, but I've seen what money can buy and what it shouldn't. I don't need more clothes. I don't need to try my luck in the stock market. I don't need a trip around the world." I pause. "I'm not saying that one wouldn't be nice, but I don't *need* it."

"Yet you 'need' to invest in my company?" he asks skeptically. "I do not mean to be looking a gift horse in the mouth, and I do not usually try to talk investors out of investing in my company"—here he shoots me a look—"but you have to admit, viewing it from my perspective, this all sounds remarkably fishy. I have the feeling there is a giant catch in there somewhere."

I nod. "You're right. There is a catch."

He raises a single eyebrow. The phone rings. He glances over at it but doesn't answer. I take it as a good sign.

"Before I tell you what the catch is, I have some questions for you. I was very impressed with several things during your presentation." I mention the research-based breakthrough he had with algae and fuel production; brackish-water production is an amazing development that he's engineered. His expression changes as he listens to me, clearly surprised that I followed what he lectured on. "But there are a few issues that you didn't address. What's your financial longevity?" It was one of the first things Delaney Cramer grilled me on when we talked. Without deep pockets, he'll be out of business in weeks, no matter how great his ideas.

I can see him make the switch, actually see him stop looking at me as a punk kid and start talking to me like an investor.

"Between a couple of government grants and three principal investors, the company has held its course," he says, clearing his throat. "The company was formed eight months ago and it has enough capital to last another six, but that's assuming I stay on a shoestring budget." He waves a hand to indicate the shabbiness of his office. As if I haven't noticed.

"What are your future financial needs?" I ask from a list of questions I prepared ahead of time.

"In order to grow, we can't realistically stay at this level. But we need to find the perfect combination of algae and output, the proverbial needle in a haystack. That takes time and money, two things that are in short supply."

The knot around my heart, the nervous cramps in my belly fade at this. I want to jump out of my seat with joy. The professor notes my relieved expression and the poor man looks both annoyed and puzzled as he sits back and crosses his arms. His eyes are dark and liquid and I'm gambling everything I've got that there's a kind soul behind them.

"What you're describing, your major obstacle to success, I know someone who could help you with it. That's the catch. My friend, the one you met the other night, he's been working on a business plan to help you get past some of those hurdles."

The astonished look on his face would be comical, if only it weren't followed by a look of visceral disgust.

"Your friend? Gavin Armand?" He shakes his head. "You know he was expelled from Tech? For cheating?"

"It's not what it seems," I quickly say. "He didn't do anything wrong."

"I will not be a part of this," he says, cutting off all discussion. My stomach twists in disappointment. Some of what I feel must show on my face, because his face softens a bit. "In my experience as a professor for many years," he says, not unkindly, "once a cheater, always a cheater. I do not need that kind of person here. I have two part-time employees. We do not have room for the deadweight or the liability of a cheater. My God, the last thing I need now is a lawsuit for patent infringement, or industrial theft or who knows what!"

"He's not a cheater! He won't steal or lie or cause you any trouble." He's clearly not convinced, and why should he believe me? I change tactics. "What have you got to lose here? He can't cheat to help you. He can't steal the business plan because it doesn't exist. Either he can pull one together or he can't. He shared some of his ideas with me and they're great. So here is the final part of my offer." Standing up, hands shoved in my pockets, I play my last card. "I'm not offering to invest a million dollars in your company, I'm offering to give it to you. A donation. Nothing in return. Not shares, not profit, not future royalties. Nothing. I don't even want my name mentioned, not to Gavin or anyone. All I ask in return is that you look at Gavin's plan. If it's not good, if it's not what you need, then you can say no thank you, and keep the money. But if it's good, you hire Gavin."

The offer shocks him.

"Why would you do that?"

I'm not ready to answer that question. "It's my money. It's my decision."

The phone rings again and this time he doesn't even glance at it.

"You're busy," I say. "I know you need to get back to work. Do we have a deal?"

The phone rings over and over. His computer beeps with incoming messages. A plane roars overhead, heading for the nearby St. Pete/Clearwater airport. I stand like a soldier, holding my breath.

"I don't accept ultimatums," he says flatly. "And I don't give second chances."

Disappointment is like lead in my veins. He won't consider looking at a business plan for a million dollars? Humiliating tears rise along with a lump in my throat. If this doesn't work, I don't know what I'm supposed to do, where I should go. I only have four days left to figure this out. For a moment, the ground yawns open under me and I sway, gripping the edge of the desk for balance.

"But," he says, and I stop my circling panic and force myself to listen, "I pride myself on having an open mind. I do not give second chances but since you claim he never cheated in the first place, I will take a look at his business plan. But do not think you can scam me, young lady. I have been teaching for fifteen years. I have seen over seven hundred students try every trick in the book."

"It's not a trick," I say stiffly. It's not Gavin he's insulting now. He's implying that I cheat too.

"Fine," he says. "But he needs to finish it soon or it's moot, regardless of our mutual misgivings," he adds, almost reluctantly. "A former 'esteemed' colleague of mine has announced he's giving a talk at the Symposium on Biofuels, Bioenergy and Biotechnology."

I look at him blankly.

"His topic is algae as fuel, and his specifics are remarkably similar to mine. He's recently formed a company called Earth-Fuel."

"Good name," I mutter.

"He's an idiot," Isakson says crisply. "But he's savvy, and as it turns out, investors are bedazzled by a slick website and glossy four-color brochures. EarthFuel is expected to announce that they have successfully grown algae in brackish water. The sudden research breakthrough is identical to mine. Apparently, one of his students has been copying my files." He presses his lips together. "So, while your infusion of cash is much needed, and your intentions seem honorable, you might as well know that in three months this company could be rendered obsolete."

Funny how he didn't mention that little gem during the fund-raiser.

"Why don't you file for a patent right now?"

"I filed for a provisional patent." He rises to face the dirty window looking out on the quiet street below, his hands on his slim hips. "It's a place holder, if you will, while I work out the exact details for the official patent. There is a one-year deadline to complete it with the exact details. My year is about to expire, right around the time of the symposium. Once it expires, everything I put in the provisional patent is public knowledge and fair game. I believe Professor Parks is simply waiting out the clock and then he will file for his own patent. But I cannot file the patent yet. It's taken me longer than I originally planned to finalize my numbers."

"Gavin's proposal can do that."

"I find that unlikely."

I hate that Isakson's bad opinion and rigid thinking about Gavin could ruin my whole plan. He's probably thinking something along the same lines, resenting a young person like me who has so much money (and therefore has power over his company) that she can dictate his actions. He must be bitter that after all his hard work, someone is about to swoop in and steal it. But, I remind myself, I might be able to fix that. I came here to buy Gavin a chance to prove his innocence to the one man whose opinion he values, and in doing so, I could save Isakson's company as well.

"You'll hear from me by Friday," I promise. It seems cosmically aligned for everything to fall into place, or fall apart, on my birthday, the day of the week that God created man.

"I look forward to it," Isakson says.

He watched her enter the building, looking so scared that he wanted to call out: "Ain't nothing gonna bite you, girl!" just to make her smile. But girls today, they didn't smile when you thought they would. They glared at you, or pretended they never heard you. Some of them yelled nasty, awful things. And there was nothing you could do because you were dirty and they were clean. So he kept his mouth shut when she walked by—she never even noticed him—but he decided, as a favor, to keep an eye on her bike.

Time had stopped having meaning for him, so he wasn't sure how long he stayed there, leaning against the wall with a clear view of the bike and the street. It couldn't have been that long. Unless he'd fallen asleep. Lately, he kept losing time. He'd have no memory of getting to a place. Be holding an empty burger wrapper with no memory of eating the burger. Sometimes he wished it were a sign that things would be over soon. Other times it scared him. A man like him can't lose track of reality like that. He had to be on guard. So he gave himself missions, like an undercover superhero. Captain Homeless. He sniggered to himself. No one ever knew they'd been protected, that they'd huddled under the shelter of his watchful eye. He chased away a car thief once. And there was one time he was sure he'd prevented a mugging. Not that anyone said thank you.

The door opened and the girl strode out. Walked out like she owned the world and had not a care in the world. Almost made you wonder if it was the same person. He eyed her suspiciously as she fiddled with the bike lock. Debated hollering at her, chasing her away so the other girl, the scared one, would have her bike when she left the building. He was still making up his mind, trying to remember what the first girl looked like, what she would say when she saw her bike was still there, that he'd protected it. Maybe she'd give him a reward. Maybe she'd invite him home so he could shower while she cooked him dinner. He smacked his lips at the thought. Struggled to his feet. But the girl was gone. No bike. No nobody. He sat back down, wondering if he'd dreamed the whole thing.

He lost time every once in a while. Woke up on a bench he'd never seen before. Said hello to people who vanished in the next instant.

Sometimes he wished things were different. Sometimes he wondered what life was like for everyone else, people who had a house and a car and a wife to cook you a big, juicy steak whenever you felt like eating one. He used to be one of those people.

He tried not to think about it.

Chapter Eighteen

I spend the rest of my morning online, looking up Professor Parks and his slick new company, EarthFuel. As I click back and forth between AlgaeGo and EarthFuel, it's obvious which one I'd invest in if I didn't know the whole story. EarthFuel's website is professional and sharp, with a simple, easy-to-understand mission statement and ambitious goals. AlgaeGo has several broken links, scientific gibberish, and a plain, almost childish home page. Isakson is totally screwed.

In the afternoon, I bike to SHCC for marine chemistry. Skipping high school is one thing. Skipping marine chemistry is another.

Plus, I need to see Gavin.

Gavin's already in his usual seat in the back, hunched over

his laptop. He only looks up when our professor begins her lecture; then our eyes meet and he nods hello. Even when I turn to face the professor, I can't stop a little smile. As the professor lectures, I sneak glances at him, but he's engrossed by whatever's on his screen. Then again, the few times he's called on, he answers brilliantly like always. The retro-T-shirt girl who was sweet to me on the beach-cleanup trip keeps rolling her eyes when Gavin talks. Maybe it's only my imagination, but she seems to be glaring at me too, though I can't imagine why.

After class, I linger in the hall until Gavin comes loping out. My heart gives a little leap when I see his tall, dark form. He grins when he sees me, his face lightening and looking younger. I wonder how much of what I'm feeling shows on my face.

"I have news," I say, practically bouncing.

"Yeah?" he asks, his voice husky. Retro-shirt girl, today wearing vintage Sprite, glares at me again. I want to tell her not to be jealous, that things aren't as simple as they look, but when I turn to say hi to her, she looks away, a sullen tilt to her head.

"Not here." I tug on Gavin's arm. "Let's go."

We head to the bike rack to grab my bike and then head to Old Farmer's Creamery, the best ice cream in the Bay. I sneak a glance at him. *I believe in you*, I remind myself. *But I'm still scared.* To cover that, I start talking.

"I was sure you'd be busted for not paying attention," I say. We've been outside less than five minutes and my skin's already beading with perspiration under the brutal sun. There's going to be a huge, wet circle where my backpack presses against me. "It's obvious you aren't taking notes. The professor's getting ticked."

"I multitask well," he says. He's sweating too. A drop of sweat forms on his temple. It rolls down the side of his face and down his neck and disappears under his thin gray shirt. The sleeves are tight around his biceps. Did he start lifting weights in juvie? Was that part of putting your boots on?

"Um . . ." I try to remember what we were talking about. "Why are you on your computer so much, anyway?"

"I'm still looking into the various property options in South Florida. There's been a lot coming on the market lately. I have an agent sending me sites to look at. Besides, I already took this class, I don't need to hear it again."

"Wait, what?" I say, confused. "If you already took it, why are you taking it again?"

His step falters for a second. He slides a sideways glance at me and gives me a little smile, like he's not sure if I'm going to be pissed or not.

"What?" My hackles rise.

"I knew you were taking it," he finally says, reluctantly. "So I signed up too."

It takes a moment for me to work through what he's saying. No one would have told him that I was taking a class at SHCC. The only way he'd know is by looking in the college's registry.

"You hacked into the SHCC database!? Oh my God, Gavin, haven't you learned anything?" I feel so many things at once, it's easiest to focus on the practicalities. "What if they find out? You'll get arrested." I leave the *again* part hanging in the air.

"They're not going to find out. I didn't touch anything. I just searched for your name," he says, oh so reasonably. Seeing my wide-eyed look, he explains, "I knew your teachers would push you toward classes here. You were brilliant at fifteen, Kohn. At seventeen, there wouldn't be anything left in high school they could teach you."

I gape for a second at the offhand compliment.

"When I saw you were enrolled for marine chemistry, I signed up. It was the only way I could think of that you'd see me."

"Idiot," I mumble under my breath, though I'm not sure if I mean him or me. "I thought it was coincidence that we bumped into each other." Actually, I thought it was divine intervention but I don't say that. "I can't believe you tracked me down like some kind of stalker, that's so creepy! Why would you do that? We barely knew each other in high school." We're in the middle of the sidewalk. Other pedestrians give us a wide berth.

"I just . . . I wanted to see you again," he says, his shoulders hunched defensively.

"You barely knew me, Gavin."

"Crap." He rakes a hand through his hair in frustration. "What I'm trying to say, badly, is that I wanted to know you. I mean, I always knew who you were, everybody knew about the brainy girl whose family won the lottery. Then your parents paid for my defense team—which, believe me, was not cheap. And when I got back to Florida, there were rumors that you guys were broke." I flush with hot embarrassment. So everyone already knows. "Leni, I don't mean it like that, I just thought maybe there was something I could help with. Not money, obviously, I'm as broke as ever, but"—he shrugs helplessly—"I wanted to get to know you a bit."

"How did you fix it so we'd have lab together?" I ask.

"I made sure to be a huge jerk at the start of the class so no one would sign next to my name."

"It does comes naturally to you."

"I didn't mean it in a creepy way," he says. "I just thought maybe we could be friends."

The sidewalk pulses with heat and matches the waves of emotions pulsing through me. I turn my head away and stare down blankly at the pavement. *Does this change anything?* I think in a panic. *Did I misread things?*

"Please, Leni. I only wanted to repay on the biggest favor of my life."

I know all about the burden of debts. I can't begrudge him the attempt to clear his. We're as intricately bound as a Celtic knot.

"Fine," I say, tightening my grip on the handlebars. "But don't ever creep around behind my back again, okay?"

"Okay," he says. "I promise. Friends?"

"Yeah," I say. "We are friends."

"Ice cream?" Gavin asks, lightening the mood.

"Make it a double."

Entering the small, wood-paneled ice cream shop, I shudder with pleasure. Even before our ice cream is scooped and tasted, my composure returns with the drop in my body temperature. Maybe it isn't a surprise that heat is the devil's domain. The cold, creamy ice cream feels like heaven after the hot, muggy air outside.

We grab a sticky wooden table near the window.

"Show me what you've been working on?" I ask.

Gavin pulls out his laptop and opens an attachment that shows aerial shots of several farmlands with large water-retention ponds scattered throughout.

"I'm looking for a site that's big enough for Isakson to set up multiple algae sites without cross contamination," he explains as he clicks through various attachments. "It needs easy road access for distribution, but still has to be close enough to the Gulf, with plenty of inland ponds, that access to brackish water isn't an issue."

"Why don't you show him what you've got so far? If he knows you're working on this, it could really change how he sees you and—"

Gavin shakes his head.

"No, I need to find the right site. Once I'm sure we have a price point we can live with and a long-term lease with favorable terms, then I'll see if Professor Isakson wants it. There's nothing to gain from going over there half-assed."

The words are assertive enough, like everything that comes out of Gavin's mouth, but there's insecurity in his voice and he isn't a guy needled much by self-doubt. It's kind of amazing that he's putting this much work into something he's half-convinced will never be used.

"But as soon as he sees your plans, even what you've got now, he's going to love it."

"You saw him on Saturday," Gavin says. He logs out and gently closes his Mac. "He doesn't trust me. He wants nothing to do with anything that's associated with me." He leaves his hands resting on the Mac for a moment, then pats it. "I know you're sold that this will change his mind, but even if that's true, I only have one shot at this. My best bet is to have everything solid, perfect and ready to go. And even then, Leni, it's a long shot."

"You should give Isakson more credit," I say bracingly, even though Gavin's right about it. I wince, remembering how the professor reacted when I made my offer. But Isakson's going to look at Gavin's program whether he likes it or not and I'd better sow some seeds of credibility.

"You know what Professor Isakson says at the start of every semester?" Gavin asks. " 'I don't give second chances.' " He mimics the professor's intonations perfectly. I heard that exact line, said exactly like that, this morning.

"Good thing you don't need a second chance," I say with false cheer. "You need an appeal process. This is your opportunity to show you never cheated in the first place. Because if you're smart enough to write this business plan and negotiate a kick-ass lease and you're willing to work this hard on a project with little chance of reward, there's no way you would cheat for a class. It isn't rational."

"Humans aren't always rational," Gavin says. When he sees the look on my face, he shrugs. "I'm just playing devil's advocate."

"Scientists are *always* rational," I say, making him laugh. "Besides, do you know where that phrase 'devil's advocate' comes from?"

He shakes his head. I didn't either until a couple of days ago but it came up as I did some useless research.

I explain as we stand up.

"When the Catholic Church examined whether a miracle happened or not, they sent special lawyers to talk to witnesses, to the doctors, whatever the situation was. As these investigators questioned the people, they pushed hard to find rational explanations for what happened. Those investigators were called the devil's advocates because they were looking to explain away a miracle." I pitch my used napkin into the trash can by the door. "You don't even need a miracle," I assure him as he holds the door open for me. The C-shaped scar on his arm stands out in relief, pale against his tanned skin. "You need a lot of hard work and a little bit of luck."

Gavin steps out after me into the heavy humidity. For a second, something sweet and vulnerable crosses his face. But he catches me watching him and the expression instantly vanishes. He manages a self-deprecating half smile and the moment passes.

"That's doable, right?"

He smiles at me, but it doesn't reach his eyes.

I grab his hand and press it hard, as if to transfer some of my certainty to him, as if to squeeze the doubts away.

The devil doesn't need any more advocates.

Gavin insists on walking me home.

"Some of those old farm sites looked really good. You must be close to finished."

"Yeah," he says. "There're a couple of properties in particular that look promising. I'll probably try to drive down there in the next couple of weeks to check 'em out in person and then if they both look good, it'll come down to who'll give the better deal."

"Don't wait a few weeks. Go tomorrow."

Gavin looks at me strangely.

"You need to get this over and done with," I say, improvising on the spot. "This is a cloud hanging over you and the sooner you finish and show it to the professor, the sooner you can move on with your life."

"That's extreme. There's a lot of negotiation that needs to take place. There's probably fifty man-hours of work left, maybe more. I could probably finish it in three weeks. . . ." He's working out the hours, his free time, but even three weeks is too late.

"My birthday is Friday," I say. "Finish it by then."

The sun disappears behind thick and dark clouds and the temperature drops ten degrees. A cool, damp wind picks up and blows my hair in my eyes. I brush it aside, afraid to break eye contact with Gavin. This is what it comes down to. Can I convince him to drive to South Florida, wrangle and negotiate on behalf of a man who thinks he's a liar, on four hours of sleep a night, tops?

He looks at me like I'm insane. Maybe I am, because I'm convinced that it all needs to come together on my birthday or it won't come together at all. Isakson will lose his company, Gavin will never clear his name, never put this behind him and never achieve any of the great things that I know he can.

"Gavin, don't sleep, if that's what it takes. It won't matter in a month or two. There's a competitor on the market, another professor from Tech. He stole Isakson's idea. If you don't help Isakson soon, you won't be able to help him at all. But if you give him the lease in four days, then he'll have a chance to test his algae out of the lab and finalize his patent before this other professor presents his work at some really prestigious conference. Or it's over," I say. "This other guy will get all the investors. He's got a fancy website, an awesome company name, and it won't matter that he's a sleazeball, or that he can't take it to the next level. As long as he files for a patent first, he's set." The words are tumbling out so fast. "If Isakson won't look at your plan with all that on the line, then you can put him behind you because it means he isn't the man you thought he was. And if that's the case, then you can move on with your life and get a degree somewhere else and forget him."

The wind stirs a flurry of dust and dried oak leaves. Knots of Spanish moss tumble against my legs.

"How do you know all this?"

"Please," I say, avoiding the question. "Will you do it?"

The sky is dark with charcoal-gray clouds, thick and low. The rising wind blows Gavin's shirt, pressing it against his chest. A big raindrop bursts on his light gray shirt, leaving a dark circle. Another falls. And another. One lands on my cheek and slides down like a tear. The patter of drops picks up.

"Your computer!" I gasp.

As if waking from a spell, Gavin jerks and grabs his laptop bag protectively. There's a bright flash of light.

"You need to get under cover," I yell.

The hustle and bustle of Fourth Street is eight blocks behind us. We're in a residential neighborhood now. We have to get indoors, fast. A loud crack of thunder booms nearby, vibrating in my chest. More people are killed by lightning in Florida than in any other state. There's more than the computer to worry about.

"Ride your bike to the ice cream shop," Gavin tells me, pushing a little at my back to hurry me.

"I'm not leaving you!"

"Then leave the bike," he yells as another crack of thunder drowns out our words.

He's right. We need to run and it'll slow us down if I push my bike along. I don't have time to lock it. The raindrops come faster and faster. I lean my bike against a lamppost. The clouds are a dark, menacing gray and when lightning flashes again, it illuminates everything like a sudden burst of white-blue sunlight. Even though I know it's coming, thunder cracks loud enough to make me jump. We only have a few minutes before the clouds open up on us. Gavin tucks his bag under his shirt and hunches over but that won't be enough to protect it. No computer could survive the drenching downpour of a Florida shower. Gavin turns to backtrack to the ice cream store, but I know someplace closer.

"Follow me!" I yell. There's a rushing sound as the wind picks up and the drops pick up their tempo.

We race down the sidewalk. I lead him through a narrow alley between two apartment buildings, not bothering to check if their lobbies are unlocked. They won't be. Not in this neighborhood. I veer to the right at the end of the alley and Gavin follows close on my heels.

The streets are deserted. Everyone else noticed the storm rolling in and found shelter. We run to a back alley with a row of metal Dumpsters, a long brick wall and a series of doors. We're both pockmarked with wet spots on our shirts and faces.

I stop in front of a metal door painted dull maroon and marked Steeped and pound on the door.

"Natasha!" I scream. "Let us in!"

Gavin pounds on the door with me, his fists making deep, rattling booms on the metal door. There's a small overhang over the back door, enough to block the light rain, but it won't be much protection once the storm is directly above us. It was a gamble to run here. If Natasha doesn't open the shop's back door, we're stuck. But as I prepare to dash around the entire building, down the connecting street and to the storefronts, the door opens and we literally stumble in.

Thunder reverberates again, the clouds burst open and rain pours down so hard and thick that visibility drops to nothing. Everything looks white. Gavin leans against the hall walls in relief and I shut the door on the storm.

It's dim in here, even after the gloom outside.

"Look what the cat dragged in," says a smug voice.

I blink as my eyes adjust. It isn't Natasha that opened the door. It's John Parker. Though he did let us in and in doing so saved Gavin's computer, I can't help feeling an uncharitable disappointment to see him.

John Parker leers at me.

I glance down and see that my shirt is wet and that it's quite obvious that I'm cold. I cross my arms defensively.

I always knew John Parker was a creep but there's something aggressive about him now that makes me grateful I didn't come in from the storm alone. Gavin picks up on it too, because he steps forward, half in front of me. That suppressed element of danger about him is suddenly not so suppressed. Gavin thrusts his hand out.

"Thanks for letting us in," he says almost pleasantly, gripping John Parker's hand. John winces and tries to pull his hand back. Gavin holds on to it for a second longer, making a point as his knuckles whiten, before letting go.

John Parker cradles his hand and looks at us sourly.

"Your sister's not here again," he accuses. "I had to open the shop by myself."

"Okay."

"She needs to tell me if she's not going to open the shop," he continues. "I can't do it all, you know." He runs his hand through his Lego-man hair, flexing his biceps, still thinking he's awesome, trying to be charming and intimidating at the same time.

"Well, John," I say coldly. "She's your boss. If you don't like it, find another job."

His lips thin with anger and then without another word, he turns and walks back to the shop. I let out a breath I wasn't aware I was holding.

"I'm thinking he wasn't a great hiring decision," Gavin says.

"You think?" I laugh, though it's really not that funny. "I don't know what my sister sees in him."

The beaded curtain still swings from where John Parker shoved past it. Gavin sneezes, pulling my attention away from John. We're both wet and cold in the air-conditioning.

"Come on," I say. "Let's see if we can find something in Natasha's office to wear."

Her office is unlocked. I root around in some old merchandise boxes and find an XL tea-shop–logo shirt for Gavin and a smaller one for me.

"Look, we're twins," I exclaim when I catch sight of us in the full-length mirror hung on the back of the door.

"Sick." Gavin shakes his head. His shirt is cream with pink lettering and mine is pink with cream letters. We match.

Our reflection in the gilt-framed mirror shows the top of my head reaching his chin. My hair is wet and has tumbled down all around my face. There's a hectic flush on my cheeks and the bridge of my nose; my eyes are bright and clear.

"I'm a mess," I say.

"You're beautiful."

"You're blind."

He barks a sharp laugh and I instinctively turn toward him because Gavin has the best laugh and it doesn't come out often. I giggle.

Florida afternoon thunderstorms, though fierce, are notoriously short-lived. By the time Gavin fires up his Mac to make sure it survived the trip, I no longer hear rain drumming on the ceiling and the last rumble of thunder was more than fifteen minutes ago.

We stay in Natasha's office another few minutes and then head out the back door again, into the dripping alley. John Parker stays in the main shop speaking with a customer.

"Do you want me to walk you home?" Gavin asks, glancing at the shut door.

"Don't worry about it. I live a few blocks away."

He looks like he's going to argue, so instead of giving him the chance, I stretch on my tiptoes and kiss his cheek. He exhales slowly, eyes closed.

"Thanks for stepping in with that creep," I say. He opens his eyes and there's so much in his gaze, it almost hurts to see it. In that moment, I know he'll do anything I ask him to. "You'll go to South Florida?" I ask.

He nods in acknowledgment. "I'll be back by Friday."

"Good luck."

Then I turn and walk away, swerving around an old man getting out of a car he parked crookedly, taking up two spots in the alley. It only takes a moment before Gavin's echoing footsteps head in the opposite direction.

I close my eyes in a quick prayer.

The trees still drip from the afternoon shower and the black asphalt steams in the afternoon sun. The grass is a new, clean sort of green, and a black cormorant stands in a grassy patch of sun, wings outstretched, looking like a totem pole topper as it dries its feathers. I pass an orange tree, its leaves glistening with raindrops. Green oranges the size of baseballs hang from its branches.

I'm a block and a half away from my house when I suddenly remember to go back for my bike.

I turn and lope, jumping over shallow puddles, running through the thin wisps of steam rising off the sidewalks. It's only been a few minutes, I reassure myself. I arrive at the street where I left my bike. I walk up and down the block, then for good measure check the next two blocks in either direction. But every lamppost I pass is empty.

My bike is gone.

Melvin watched as the youngsters on the sidewalk separated. He figured the air around them might combust with all the heat and fireworks those two were putting out. He might be eighty-six years old but he wasn't dead yet. Looking at them, so young and fresh, full of piss and vinegar, made him feel tired. A little wistful too. Oh, the fights he and Betty would get into some days. Neighbors three doors down could hear their shouting—you'd have thought the world was coming to an end.

He smiled a little. Of course, their reconciliation . . . well, sometimes they'd fight just to have a reason to make up afterward.

Betty died eight years ago this October. It was hard to believe she'd been gone so long. Oh, how he missed her.

His daughter, Sally, kept telling him he should sell the condo, move closer to her. But what did he want with Connecticut? He'd lived there for sixty years. Snow and ice. People in too damn much of a hurry. There was a reason he and Betty retired down south. Sally always was too bossy for her own good. Now that her youngest was out of the house, she must be feeling bored, to start in on him. He'd stick with Florida. It was the last place he and Betty lived together, and the only way he was leaving the condo was feet first.

Still, he wasn't doing so bad for an old fart. There were several

195

lady friends who invited him to dinner on a regular basis. He knew each one hoped to be the new Mrs. Franklin, but although he was happy enough to eat their home cooking and take them to a show or a lecture, he knew that he would never marry again. There was only one Mrs. Franklin and she was resting in Connecticut.

He looked over his shoulder at the two whippersnappers and shook his head. To have the energy for those emotions, well, sometimes he was glad he was eighty-six and sometimes he wished he were twenty-six again. What he wouldn't give to get to do it again. Not to do things differently, but to be in the thick of it again.

"Good luck to you," he said to the empty street. "It goes by faster than you can imagine."

Chapter Nineteen

I'm annoyed by the haunted-mansion creak of the rusty hinges on the front door, annoyed by my wet shoes squeaking on the marble, and completely pissed off at the thief who stole my bike. I had that bike for four years. Getting to school would be a real pain now.

As usual, no one's up and about.

I stomp off to the kitchen for something to eat but our walk-in pantry looks worse than usual. Because it's so large, the rows and rows of bare shelves seem like a post-apocalyptic grocery store. There's an ancient can of baking powder; several mostly empty bags of rice; a dusty tin of smoked oysters that must have come in a gift basket years ago when my parents still gave and received things like that. Lately my mom's been getting weird things at the store, food we don't usually eat. Canned hominy.

Powdered potatoes. Golden Puffs cereal. Grape jelly, though none of us like it. But even those odd foods have been devoured. I check the fridge for leftovers, but someone must have gotten to them already. In our giant stainless steel Sub-Zero French-door refrigerator with the freezer on the bottom, there's a door full of condiments, a tub of ancient cream cheese and a half-empty jar of salsa.

Hoping that my mom is out at the grocery store, I end up boiling rice, mixing jasmine, white and basmati because there isn't enough of any one for a full serving. After a quick sniff and a shrug, I dump the salsa in with the rice. What cooks up won't ever be served at any self-respecting restaurant, but I'm pleased enough with it. It's filling and comforting in the way that warm mush can be. I take it outside, even though it's prime time for the mosquitoes to be out, and sit on the back patio watching the water.

Everything will be different soon.

I push my half-empty bowl aside and hug my knees. The seat cushions are still wet from the afternoon shower and the damp seeps into my shorts.

What will my parents say when I tell them the money's gone? I don't know what we'll do, where we'll go. But with every second that ticks by, we're traveling closer to a cataclysmic event for our family. I wish it were already over and done with, that I was already on the other side, eighteen years old and living with the fallout. Will they hate me?

I force myself to leave my spot on the patio and to start solving one of the smaller problems in my life. My wheels. I ride my bike to high school, to SHCC, to practically everywhere that's too far to walk.

Someone in the family might have bought a bike at some point. My mom could have in a fit of wishful exercise thinking. Or Eddie might have if he had visions of triathlons dancing in his head. It's possible. He has enough footballs and basketballs slowly deflating and gathering dust that it's just as likely there's a bike slowly rusting into oblivion in the frightful nightmare of our garage. There's an easy way to find out.

The punishing heat in the dim garage immediately has me sweating. When we first moved in, my dad talked about installing an AC unit for the three-car garage, but that project fell by the wayside. Currently there's barely enough room for my mom's car to park on the far left of the garage. Which isn't actually a problem since my dad sold his car five months ago. Eddie's lease was repossessed after he missed four payments.

I hate going in the garage. There's thousands of dollars' worth of stuff in here, but there's a lot of crap too, all jumbled together. Even the items that are still good are grimy with cobwebs and roach scat. The garage is the sad and shameful graveyard where the fun times we thought we'd have came to rot and die.

But bikes are big. It shouldn't be too hard to figure out if there's one in here.

I poke my way past gallons of half-used paint; boxes bursting with holiday decorations, wrapping paper and school projects; an old rusted push mower, three tires, two TVs. There's our dining-room set from the old house and two dressers that used to be in Natasha's room before she redid it. It reeks in here too, which makes me wonder if some citrus rats have moved in. There could be a whole family nesting somewhere in the garage and who would know? My dad's workshop is in a corner of the garage. He jerry-rigged a small AC unit to keep him from being flambéed during the summer. His corner holds all sorts of odds and ends and the beginnings of several types of small engines, none of them completed or functioning.

Bike, I remind myself. But after half an hour, dripping with sweat and covered in crud, I haven't found one.

Eddie's probably awake by now. It's time to stop this ridiculous search and ask him if he ever bought a bike.

I hear the TV before I even reach his room.

"You decent?" I call out before opening the door.

ESPN is on and Eddie is probably still in bed. I hesitate for a moment. I reeeeally don't want to walk in on my brother if he's not dressed. If he didn't hear me because of the TV, there's no guessing what state he's in. As a safety precaution, I shut my eyes.

"Eddie?" I call out loudly from the doorway. "Is it safe?"

"Stop shouting, you idiot," he says. "Come in." Then his voice drops to a growly rumble. "If you dare."

I crack open my eyelids. He's in bed wearing a T-shirt. The rest of him is covered by his bedspread. Good enough. The blinds are drawn across his window to facilitate TV watching, which is ironic because Eddie's room has one of the best views in the house.

"Somebody stole my bike," I announce, perching on the edge of his bed. It smells in here too, all musty and sweaty. He hasn't changed his sheets in a long time. There's no maid anymore and my mom won't enter his room. Not that my mom should be doing Eddie's laundry. By the time each of us turned fifteen, my mom declared the statute of Mom-doing-your-laundry-for-you expired. At twenty-seven, Eddie seems to be challenging that. Grease-stained fast-food bags are crumpled on the floor near the bed like used tissues.

"Your room is disgusting," I say. "You need to clean it up."

"You volunteering? Or doesn't it count unless I have gills?"

"It doesn't count when you have two hands of your own that can pick up a freakin' broom."

"Thanks for the tip, Mom," he says. Then he belches and turns the volume up on the TV. "Well, if that's everything, sorry about your bike. . . ."

"No, Eddie." I don't mean to fight with him. In fact, I can't, since he won't ever fight back. "I need a bike. I was wondering if you had an old one somewhere I could borrow."

He blinks slowly and then turns away from the TV to face me.

"You're asking if you can borrow my bike?" he asks incredulously.

"Yeah." I shrug uncomfortably under his stare. "Why is that so crazy?"

"Leni," he says. "You realize that I haven't left this house in over a year?"

"Um, I . . ." To my mortification, I find I didn't realize it. My cheeks heat up in shame. Now that he's said it, I suddenly see it's true. He might as well have been under house arrest. I try to cover for this gross inattentiveness. "I didn't know if you'd bought one a while back and weren't using it. . . ." How could I have missed it? He's my brother and we live in the same house but I was so grossed out by his slovenly gluttony and the constant TV that I really hadn't seen past that to the state he'd sunk to.

I look down, unable to meet his eyes.

"No," he says quietly. "I don't have a bike you can borrow. Sorry."

"Eddie," I say, reaching out for his hand. It's hot and fleshy. I squeeze it, sighing deeply. "I'm sorry. I didn't realize."

"Don't worry, kid," he says, surprisingly kind. "I didn't advertise. Sometimes I don't even think Mom and Dad have figured it out. Seriously, though, why do you need to borrow a bike? You're getting a truckload of money on Friday. Buy your own freakin' bike. By the time the credit-card bill comes, you can buy the whole damn store."

I hesitate, but then decide I might as well get a preview of what's coming my way.

"I'm not keeping the money," I say softly, whispering the secret of the century. You might think with the TV blaring playbacks, and with his perpetual groggy stare, that Eddie might have missed my meaning, but his bloodshot eyes pop wide open and he sits up in bed.

"What. The. Hell?" There's a spark there of the Eddie I know, the mischievous trickster who loves nothing more than a good joke. "Are you serious?"

"Serious as an oil spill."

He flops back in bed dramatically, making me bounce up and down, a dingy in the wake of a carrier.

"I know it's going to make life harder on you." I sweep my arms to indicate the room, the house. "It's going to be rough for all of us."

"You taking my advice?" he says, arms outflung, staring at the ceiling, not seeing it. "You gonna party in Bali?"

I shake my head, even though he's not looking at me. "No, that's not what I'm doing."

He struggles to sit up again and stares at me with dull-eyed disappointment.

"Don't tell me, you're going to give all your money away to some tree-hugging group that claims it can save the world?" he says, shaking his head. "You're something else, Leni."

"No. Not that either. Not that I wasn't tempted. But I'm doing something a bit different. I'm fixing something that broke. And sometimes a lot of money can do things nothing else can."

"Like what?" He tilts his head in question. *Like a miracle,* I think. He's not yelling. He's not calling me names or telling me what a horrible person I am to do this to the family. That's actually a lot better than I expected. He's shocked, true, but in a weird way, he's intrigued. Which is good, I can work with intrigued.

"It can buy an innocent person a second chance," I tell him.

He's quiet for a moment.

"You really think your money is going to do that?"

"It's a gamble," I say, with more honesty than I planned on.

"It could be a huge mistake. But I saw how Mom and Dad spent their money, and how you did and Natasha did, and no offense, but none of that turned out to be such a great thing either."

"Oh, you're wrong," he says. "It was great while it lasted. It was abso-freaking-lutely great."

"While it lasted," I finish for him. "I guess I'm shooting for abso-freaking-lutely great even after it's all gone."

"Good luck with that." Then he laughs with a sort of rusty guffaw. "Not that it wouldn't be something to see."

"Yeah." I smile, but I'm so sad on the inside. He is in there amid the ruins, my funny, loyal brother. "That would be great, wouldn't it?"

To my surprise, he smiles. "Leni, I have to hand it to you, I didn't think you'd have the balls to say no to Mom and Dad," he says. "Good for you, kid." In a weird way, having his approval makes me feel like the burden isn't as heavy as I thought.

"I almost didn't," I admit. "It makes me sick to let them down. But honestly, I don't think the money was going to fix that many of our problems anyway. We might as well deal with all this now instead of later, you know?"

"I don't know, dealing with crap is usually better later instead of sooner in my book."

I give the trashed room a pointed look. "Yeah, I noticed."

He doesn't bother replying to that. Sitting in the middle of his rumpled, lived-in, king-size bed, he looks like nothing more than a giant overgrown slug. He even has a cowlick sticking up in the back like an antenna.

"Who is it?" he asks.

We both know what he's asking. I debate not telling him. I

wonder if this should be a secret, anonymous, like Gavin's accuser at Tech. But then I think, *Screw it, I'm not using the devil's tactics.*

The phone rings somewhere in the house; we both ignore it. "It's Gavin Armand."

The words drop like a bomb in the room, blowing away the excitement, the good feeling. His face freezes at the name and I shiver at the sudden change in Eddie's mood. Eddie was here for the arrest and trial. At the time, I didn't pay much attention to my older brother—I was rather self-involved with high school drama. I do remember he was on the periphery, leaning on the doorjamb in the kitchen, listening in on the latest development, the most recent setback. The sudden anger on his face at Gavin's name tells me that I've been clueless about my brother in a lot of ways.

"So you're saying he didn't really hack into the DMV to sell people's Socials?"

"He did," I say. "But he got kicked out of Tech for nothing, that's the part that wasn't fair." When I say it like that, it doesn't actually sound very compelling. "What I mean," I quickly say, "is that someone robbed him of his second chance. And with his background, no one will ever give him another one. You should have seen it when we bumped into his old professor. He was so ugly to him. That's what it's going to be like for the rest of his life, everyone judging him, thinking he's beneath them. Gavin's really smart. He can literally make the world a better place."

"You've lost your mind," Eddie says. "That creep was convicted. Of defrauding. The government. Remember? Why the hell would you want anything to do with him?" It's the first time Eddie's been angry at me in years and I shrink back from him. "Just because some hot guy asks you to spend a million dollars on him, you do it?" He shakes his head with disgust. "What the hell is wrong with you?"

"Gavin didn't ask for it," I say, stung and defensive. "He doesn't even know I'm doing anything for him." I tell myself Eddie's anger comes because he loves me and doesn't want me to get scammed, but there's something in his tone, some deep contempt that feels very personal and hurtful. "And I don't have a crush on him. What is with you and Dad? We're not dating."

"You are a fool," Eddie says, his lip curled. "You are a pathetic little fool. You and Natasha." His eyes narrow, disdain dripping from his words. "What is wrong with you two? You don't know how to let a guy go, do you?"

It's a below-the-belt blow and even Eddie looks a little sick after he says it. I can barely hold back the words that want to tumble out, to the point that I break out in a light sweat, a combination of anger and mortification. It won't help to stoop to his level, to fling a few choice insults in his direction about all the clever choices he's made in his life.

"Anyway," I say, rising from his bed, wiping my damp hands on my shorts. "That's why I need to find a bike to borrow. I'll be as broke on Friday as I am today. Actually, more broke because I won't have a trust fund."

"Don't do it, Leni," my brother says. His face is puffy and gray. He has dark bags under his eyes and he suddenly looks exhausted. "You're making a huge mistake. You're going to regret it."

My stomach twists at the cold pronouncement. Am I? Is this a huge mistake?

"I'm sorry you feel that way," I say. "I think you wasted your money too, not that you ever asked me. I love you, but I'm not asking you for permission. I'm just telling you where the money is going." The bowl of warm mush I ate an hour ago slowly turns on me, no longer comforting. "I'd appreciate it if you didn't tell anyone else. Okay?"

He hesitates and for an awful moment I think he's going to say, *No, I'm not keeping this a secret.* But in the end, he nods, looking sick and miserable, and I leave his room feeling as bad as he looks. Turning to shut the door behind me, I catch a glimpse of him as he grabs a mug from his nightstand and hurls it viciously against the wall. The mug isn't empty. It breaks with a loud crack and liquid splatters on the floor.

I close the door behind me with a soft click.

It doesn't matter, it doesn't matter, I repeat to myself, a litany, a mantra. It doesn't matter what Eddie thinks. He doesn't understand. Who is he to cast stones, sitting in his disgusting room? He doesn't know the full story.

Even though it's all true, I can't ignore the fact that his bad reaction means there's going to be a hell of an explosion when my parents find out. And he wasn't even upset that I wasn't giving them the money—he only flipped when he found out who it was for. *Dear God*—I rub my temple, swallowing back the panic—*please let this be the right thing.*

I wait a bit in the dim hall, my ears straining, all my senses reaching out, searching for anything, a hint, a feeling, something that will tell me God is listening, that Michael is with me like he promised, that I'm doing the right thing. My heartbeat and its echoing thrum of blood whooshes through my veins. I isolate the headache to a pulsing pain behind my right eye, a favorite spot for stress headaches. On one of the websites I stumbled across, the archangel Michael, God's right hand, was described as the intercessor, our heavenly advocate, who pleads the case for (stupid, wicked, dense) mankind before our creator.

Maybe that's where he is now, trying to buy me more time before my personal judgment day. Breathing quietly calms me, my heartbeat slows down, my nerves steady a bit. But that's about it. There's no one in this house except me and my messed-up family.

Chapter Twenty

Sometime around midnight, Natasha slides into bed with me. I wake up from a deep sleep with a start to find her lying next to me, reeking of smoke, beer and sweat.

"Natasha." My heart pounds with the sudden shock of finding her in bed with me. "Are you okay?"

Natasha lies flat on her back, staring at the canopy, only a pale blob in the darkness. I push back my sleep-tousled hair, thinking she's going to speak. But she stays silent, looking and acting like a corpse. I guess that's her answer.

"I was at the shop today," I say, though I know it'll be useless. "John Parker really shouldn't be your assistant manager. He shouldn't even work at the shop. Something's not right about him."

"The devil always wins," Natasha whispers. Her breath is rank and her words have a sibilant hiss. "You think he's not watching. But he is. You think you're smarter. But you're not."

I shiver, though the night is warm and the AC hasn't kicked in. The ceiling fan turns in slow, creaky circles, barely churning any breeze. My skin is damp and sticky with sweat, my hair clinging to my face. I push the strands away and turn to look at her.

"What does that have to do with John Parker?" I try for a reasonable tone, although she's freaking me out. I resist the urge to open my closet, to look under the bed. That's not where the monster is hiding. "You hired him," I remind her, stubbornly sticking to this less freaky topic. "So demote him. Or better yet, fire him."

"It's too late."

"Are we still talking about John Parker?"

"Leni . . ." Natasha sits up suddenly and cups my face between her clammy, skeletal hands. I instinctively jerk away, feeling trapped. Tears well in her bloodshot eyes and she curls her hands into fists and hugs them to her chest. "I know I seem awful to you," she says. "And if you can't forgive me, then no one can."

"Tell me what happened," I urge. "You need to talk about it."

But she mutely shakes her head.

She's living in hell and I have to be patient. I can hear the promise I said out loud in this room, on this bed. *I will fix it.* And before I know it, I say it out loud once more. "I will fix it."

There's a small choking sound as Natasha starts crying again. Maybe with relief. Then I realize she isn't crying.

Natasha's laughing at me.

"Baby, you can't fix this," she says, her teeth and eyes glowing white in the dark. "No donation to Greenpeace, not a thousand hours of community service, no recycling program is going to fix this." Her face is pale with dark sunken eyes, and even in this sad state, she's condescending and superior. "Sometimes we lose. Sometimes we just screw up beyond all measure."

"Stop, Natasha." I grab her arm. "Just stop!"

"You were right, Leni," she says, ignoring my tight grip. "You're right to hate me."

"I love you, Natasha. You're my sister. I could never hate you."

"Do you know what he said to me? He said, 'I can't make anyone do anything, baby girl.'" Her intonation is different, deeper, and I realize she's mimicking him. "'It's that whole free-will bullshit.' That's the part that gets me, Leni," she says brokenly. "The devil can't *make* anyone *do* anything. Which means I chose this goddamn awfulness. I chose to win millions. And I chose to . . ." She shakes her head. "But after, after I did what he told me, I had to stop and vomit. Because who would choose this?" Her voice cracks. "Who *chooses* that?"

She turns until she's curled on her side, her knees pressed to her chest in a fetal position.

"I don't hate you," I say again.

"You should," she says simply. "I do."

The next morning she's gone and no one else in the house even knew she came. I'd doubt my own mind, except for the long dark red hairs curled on the pillow next to mine. Besides, the room smells a little like clove cigarettes. It all renews my determination. I have to get rid of this money and I have to do it right.

The professor's office suite is no less shabby and no more populated than it was two days ago. This time, I head straight to the closed door in the back and knock loudly.

"Who is it?" Isakson asks curtly.

"Leni Kohn."

He looks up from his computer in exasperation as I open the door.

"Again?"

"I wanted to update you," I say. "You'll receive the plan on Friday. That's in two days," I add unnecessarily. In my darker moments, I pictured him turning down the money and Gavin's help out of sheer obstinacy. "You'll give Gavin a chance to show you what he's been working on, right?" My anxiety has been growing as my birthday looms. Isakson has to recognize the value of the proposal immediately; there's no time for a gradual understanding of its implications. His annoyed expression doesn't reassure me.

"We have a deal," I remind him tersely. "You said it wasn't giving him a second chance, remember? You said you were keeping an open mind."

"I remember what I said."

"He has been haunted by what happened to him at Tech," I blurt out, desperate to break through that indifferent, annoyed expression. "Someone framed him and he never knew why. He didn't fight the charges, which if you knew him, you'd know that's not normal, he fights for everything. When we were in high school, he never accepted what people told him, he always pushed back. Did you know he was in juvie?" I demand. "He got through it because he never backed off from a fight. No one respects you if you back off from a fight." Gavin said that life is like juvie, only less brutal. And I suddenly realize he's exactly right. Isakson doesn't respect him, doesn't believe in him, because Gavin never "put his boots on." "Maybe he was tired of fighting," I say, heatedly, "or maybe he didn't think he would win, but I can promise you, it wasn't because he was guilty."

The professor studies me, his face impenetrable. I'd give half my million to know what he's thinking. He tugs at his beard and seems about to speak. I don't give him a chance.

"He doesn't know my money has anything to do with you looking at his business model, if that's what you're thinking. That's not why he's doing it. And I don't want him to ever know. Okay? None of this matters if he thinks you were paid off."

A look of outrage crosses Isakson's face.

"Just so we're clear," I bluster, kicking myself. I'm only making the situation worse.

"Crystal," Isakson bites out. "You have a lot of faith in your friend. How long have you known him?"

"We met a few years ago, at the Citrus Park High science magnet program."

"I presume this was before he was arrested, tried and convicted for thwarting federal immigration policy by hacking into the DMV, selling hundreds of Social Security numbers, and establishing a professional-grade scheme that had hackers around the country sitting up and taking notice?"

Oh. So he knew about that.

"Yes," I say faintly. "That's when we lost touch for a bit."

"Young lady, I don't care how much money you have, a million dollars is a ridiculous amount of money. This might be against my best interests but someone needs to tell you to think this over very carefully. Think twice before throwing it away on someone like that."

"I'm not 'throwing it away.' I'm investing it in a great company," I say, feeling my chin rise in challenge and my face heat up in embarrassment. "Besides, money isn't everything."

"Only someone with a lot of money says that."

I don't bother answering him.

We're clearly at a stalemate. He thinks I'm a naïve fool, blowing my money. I think he's a close-minded elitist, quick to pass judgment.

Finally, the professor nods. "If he brings in the plan, I promise to be fair. I'm always fair," he says with a flinty look. "For your sake, I hope you're putting your faith in the right person."

"We agree on that," I say. "See you on Friday."

Gavin doesn't show up for class that afternoon. Hopefully, he's in South Florida touring properties and hammering out a deal with a landowner, who may or may not end up having a lease for Isakson to sign at the end of the week.

I'm counting down to my birthday in hours now, not days.

I find myself praying at regular intervals. While waiting for the light to change. Washing my hands. Losing track of the SHCC professor's lecture.

Am I doing the right thing? Please. Is this right?

But there's nothing. Not a word. Or a sign. Not even a hunch. There's no gut feeling to follow. I'm going to devastate my parents. Eddie says it's a horrible idea. Natasha says it's a lost cause. Professor Isakson says my trust is misplaced. And Gavin doesn't even know what I'm planning to do.

Please, tell me if this is what you meant?

But he doesn't. They don't.

I wouldn't be doing this if it weren't for you, I accuse Michael. *Why can't you tell me if this is what you meant?*

With all my ferocious prayers and furrowed brows, all I manage to do is get odd looks from the other students in class.

I text Gavin to see what's going on. But he only sends a quick reply that there's nothing to report yet.

I need to believe in redemption. I need to believe that people who make mistakes get second chances. That people who suffer great wrongs also reap unexplained benefits. That there is balance in the world and that I help bring it.

I don't hear from Michael or anyone else but that doesn't stop me from praying. *Please let this be right.*

In the end, even though no one responds from above, there is something.

Despite the deafening silence from the powers that be, even without the confirmation that would set my soul at ease, I'm determined to continue moving forward in the direction I have chosen. Because my decision is right. Right in the fullest sense of the word: selfless, kind, far-reaching and well thought out.

I need courage to give away my trust fund.

I need conviction.

To my surprise, I find that I have what I need after all.

Chapter Twenty-One

It's a beautiful Florida evening. The heat of the day has dissipated and the cool, salty breeze coming off the bay clears the air. The clouds are wearing their ridiculous sunset colors: citrus orange, coral pink, the sky a neon blue behind them, more fitting to the inside of the Salvador Dali Museum down the street than anything else. The epitome of a passing trend, the colors only last a few minutes before fading. The clouds take off their makeup, ask for a refund and return to being normal, rather drab particles of moisture in the lower atmosphere. They're not even white as the sunlight fades, but a dirty, muddled sort of grayish-brown, mousy women under those flashy showgirl clothes. I stand by the giant banyan tree across the street from Steeped and watch the colors dim, a little reminder from above that nothing lasts.

My birthday is tomorrow.

"It was a good show," I tell them. "Lovely while it lasted." A woman wearing a bathing suit and a neon-yellow terry-cloth cover-up gives me a strange look and a wide berth as she passes me. I've become a typical Florida weirdo, talking to myself.

Steeped is empty, though my sister is inside, tallying up the day's receipts.

There is an old Jewish teaching that a person should keep two scraps of paper in his pockets. On one scrap, he should write *God created the whole world for me*. In the other pocket, he should keep a scrap that says *I am nothing but dust*. Because both of these statements are true and one shouldn't forget either.

I take a deep breath and cross the street. The silver bell tinkles merrily as I enter the shop. Natasha looks up from the back of the store. She's wearing baggy jeans and an old, loose shirt. Her hair is pulled in a severe bun and her complexion is alarmingly sallow. Her eyes are sunken and feverish.

"I'm doing it," I say softly. "I'm giving it all away."

She takes a sharp breath at the news and her chin quivers as she fights to keep her composure. "You are?"

"I'm giving someone the chance to save themselves. And he will. They both will." If I say it with enough conviction, maybe it'll actually come true.

"Oh," she chokes out. There's gratitude, relief and jealousy in that one smothered cry. "Who?"

"You remember Gavin Armand?" She nods. "A former professor of his is starting a new company for alternative fuel.

It's kind of a long story. But it's the right thing to do. I'm sure of it."

I am struck by how different we must look to an outsider. Natasha, with slumped shoulders and a haggard face, and me, standing tall and pleased with myself.

"I'm sorry, Natasha." I reach for her hand because she looks so sad and I don't know what will ever take that haunted look away. "What are you going to do?"

She shrugs and looks around her shop.

"I'm losing the store, you know," she says matter-of-factly.

"What!" I exclaim. "Why?"

"It's bleeding money. There's no way I can keep it."

"But it's doing great. There're always customers and it won Best of the Bay." I shake my head in confused surprise. "I don't get it. How long has this been going on?" I can't imagine Natasha without her tea shop.

"It doesn't matter," she says. "It's not like I could have kept it after everything." She looks away. "Anyway, I'm glad you found the courage to do it. I was worried you'd feel like you had to give the money to Mom and Dad." Her fingers are bony and cold in mine. "I'm proud of you for doing the right thing."

"Thanks, Natasha." My heart wrenches as I squeeze her hand. "I never would have given it away if you hadn't first told me I should. You're the one that started me thinking about it."

She nods, accepting the thanks, her part of the good deed.

"Go on," she says, letting go of my hand and giving me a little push in the direction of the shop's front door. "Go home.

I'm sure Mom and Dad are waiting for you. I'm going to close for the night anyway."

It's growing darker by the minute and my parents always want me back by dark on a school night. I hug Natasha fiercely.

"I love you," I tell her. She kisses my forehead.

On my way out, I grab a weekly paper to read at home. I'm not quite halfway home when I hear my name.

Leni.

"What?" I turn around.

Leni.

In a sudden rush of prickles, I realize I didn't hear my name called. I felt it.

My heart hammers wildly in my chest and my eyes must look crazy.

Go back, Leni. The voice is urgent now. *Hurry.*

I pivot on my heel and throw the paper down as I sprint back to the store. The fluttering sheets of newsprint scatter like pigeons behind me.

Once I reach the store, the initial panic that had me running escalates into full-blown dread. The front door is still unlocked, and I push in, the bell tinkling weakly. In that first moment, everything seems fine, just like I left it.

Then I smell smoke.

"Natasha!" I shout. "Natasha, where are you?"

The smell is stronger and sharper the farther I go into the shop. I cough as I call out her name. "Natasha!"

The bathroom door flies open and my sister comes tumbling out.

"We have to get out of here!" I yell. She looks disoriented. I left the store not ten minutes ago.

Smoke slips between the beaded strips of the curtain. For a moment, my sister freezes, horror and shock on her face. I run to her and grab her roughly by the arm, tugging her out.

"No!" she says, fighting me. "I have a fire extinguisher in the back, I can put out the fire!"

"It's too late," I cry. "We have to get out of here."

There's a sudden roar and flames explode forward, as if gunning for us. There's a horrifying beauty to the licks of fire that glide like snakes across the ceiling and walls. Flames race enveloping the shop and shelving as merchandise bursts into flames. The heat is unbearable. In a dim part of my mind, I wonder why my skin isn't burning, it's that hot.

Natasha screams and I pull hard on her arm. We race toward the front of the shop, stumbling in panic over chairs and tables. The fire is all around us, spreading faster and faster, consuming everything in its path. Heavy black smoke gathers at the ceiling, growing thicker and lower with each second. Has it even been two minutes since I entered the store? We are inside a hurricane of fire. Every time we fall, inhuman strength has me standing up again, pulling my nearly limp sister along with me. Red, gold and blue-green flames dance all around us, but by some miracle, none of them touch us directly. In the middle of an intense adrenaline rush, maybe some weird mental coping mechanism, all I feel is a cool breeze at my back, pushing me forward.

We reach the front of the shop and I throw us both through the door. We tumble outside, landing heavily on the ground.

There are already sirens wailing, and a small crowd of bystanders gasp as we fall out of the store.

"Are you all right?" someone asks me, crouching down. I gulp for air, unable to speak. I don't understand how Natasha and I made it out of the store. "Where's the other person?" the woman asks, her face scrunched in concern as she scans the street around us.

"What?" I'm fighting to catch my breath, gulping the blessedly cool, clean air. I barely register what she's babbling about.

"It's okay. There wasn't anyone else inside," Natasha rasps. "Just us."

There's a small explosion inside the store and people scream in surprise. The crowd takes a prudent step back. The lady crouching next to us helps Natasha and me stand. We scramble back from the burning shop. The heat is horrible, even standing outside.

I bend over, racked with a deep hacking cough that hurts my lungs.

"The ambulance is on its way, dear," she says, hovering over me, wanting to help but unsure how. I couldn't believe my eyes when I saw you through the glass window with the fire all around you. Then the three of you came bursting out that door. I don't know how you made it out alive."

I don't want to think about how close we came to dying, so I focus on the one part of the question that I can easily correct.

"My sister and I were the only ones inside," I say, once I catch my breath.

"It's the darndest thing." She shakes her head in confusion, looking between my sister and me. "I really could have sworn there were three people as you burst out the door."

Natasha sinks to her hands and knees as she vomits in the gutter. The woman turns to her in concern, our conversation forgotten.

I suddenly understand. I don't say anything, but in my heart, I realize she's right.

"Oh, Michael," I whisper, my body shaking in delayed reaction. The fire roars in fury behind me—a burning fiery furnace. Standing a hundred feet away, I feel the heat baking my back. And lo, we have no hurt.

Thank you, I mouth silently. Protector indeed. *Thank you— thank you—thank you.*

The first of the firefighters pull up and quickly connect a hose to the long fire truck and begin spraying the fire. A second truck pulls up behind the first and connects a line between the fire hydrant and the first engine to refill its tank. Other firefighters lead people away from the sidewalk.

The woman glances at the store again, shakes her head again, and lets herself be led away.

Soon there's an ambulance and a couple of police cars parked in the street.

The EMTs check us over, but it's clear that we're fine, not a scratch on us. The police are next—they want to get a statement. Everything takes so long. The fire's mostly out by the time they finish taking my statement. Meanwhile, the fire marshal and the police have been busy conferring.

By the look on their faces when they start talking to Natasha, it isn't going to go well.

"You're the owner, huh? How's business been lately?"

The questions take on a hostile tone. It seems the fire spread unusually fast. Unnaturally fast. The fire investigator suspects an accelerant. The sprinklers never engaged, which is highly suspicious. Natasha was the only one in the store.

I didn't even stop to think about how the fire started or why it spread so fast.

"They think I did it," Natasha says to me when the officer steps away. "They think I torched my own shop for the insurance money."

"Did you?" I ask, unable to stop myself.

"No! I would never do that. I was almost killed! If you hadn't come back, I don't think I would have made it out of there alive."

She's right. She was in the bathroom, oblivious to the danger. Plus, she wanted to put out the flames. Those aren't the actions of an arsonist.

"Who would burn your shop down?"

She presses her lips together, unable or unwilling to say.

John Parker's malicious face comes to mind. There was more wrong with him than simple greediness.

"Do you think . . . ," I say hesitantly, looking over my shoulder. "Do you think someone was, um"—it's awkward to say this—"paying back a favor that they owed?"

She knows what I mean exactly.

"I don't know, Leni," she says tiredly. "But they did a crack job if that's what it was. I was the only one in the store, the only one with something to gain—the owner of a failing store. It doesn't look good. It's called insurance fraud, and people go to jail for it."

She doesn't sound scared. She sounds resigned.

"You're innocent," I protest. "You didn't set your store on fire."

"Leni," she says, "I haven't been innocent since I was seventeen."

Chapter Twenty-Two

I wake up Friday morning and I am eighteen.

The police let Natasha go without booking her, warning her not to leave town until the fire marshal finished his investigation. She told my parents about the fire, but not that she's the police's prime suspect at the moment.

I didn't get home until nearly midnight. Neither one of my parents could stop touching us, as if to continually double-check that we did, in fact, survive the fire unscathed. It was something the firefighters were suspicious about, actually. How could we have gotten out so quickly without prior knowledge of the fire?

I come downstairs and find that my mom left me a birthday note on the kitchen island. My parents left early this morning to help Natasha go through the store to figure out if anything is salvageable.

Happy birthday, sweetheart. We love you so much! PS Don't worry about your party. I'll email everyone to come to the house instead. And check the foyer!

My mom doodled a little sketch of a butterfly and a blossom in each corner. Roots and wings, what she and my dad always said they wished to give us. I fold the note and slip it in my pocket, something to keep for later when they aren't speaking to me. The fire from last night has only strengthened my resolve, though it'll make it that much harder on my parents. Now none of us will have anything left from the win.

I pad out to the foyer in bare feet and stop at the sight of a gorgeous, gleaming new bicycle parked in the middle of the marble entryway. There's a giant bow stuck between the handlebars. It's a beach cruiser, pale blue with white trim, with thick tires that can ride on sand. It's not a fast bike, but there's a basket in the front, a little silver bell, and a wide, cream-colored seat that looks comfortable enough to lounge on and watch TV.

It's my perfect bike.

I sigh.

I return to the kitchen with a heavy heart. My mom must have gone to the store yesterday, because there's fresh milk in the fridge and cereal in the pantry. I fix a bowl and force myself to eat. My heart is beating too fast, my palms are clammy. I'm nauseated with nerves. Every kind of worst-case scenario flies through my mind. The best I can come up with is that it'll be over by this evening. There's that to look forward to.

* * *

227

For the second time in a week, and the second time in my high school career, I skip school.

The attorney who manages my trust fund opens her office at nine. I'm at the darkened glass doors by eight-thirty with nothing to do but wait. An ambulance wails. Cars on their morning commute rumble down the street. Life, passing me by. There's a part of me expecting something to happen. Some unnatural disaster, the devil, running interception. A part of me hopes for it. I'm ready for a fight. I'm itching for one. A mugger, perhaps. A sudden hailstorm that knocks down the power grid. Bring it on.

But there's nothing.

I keep my weight on the balls of my feet, my arms loose and ready by my side, my eyes alert and scanning my surroundings—everything my ex–Special Forces survival instructor taught me, back during my parents' fear-of-kidnapping stage. An elderly man, walking toward his regular coffee shop, looks startled at the just-try-it-buddy glare I give his friendly nod.

The air grows hot and humid. Other than a couple of mosquitoes, nothing bothers me. A great blue heron walks by, its stilt-like legs giving it a cautious gait, like someone picking their way across the floor after a glass shatters. It's almost as tall as I am, with slate-blue feathers, bright yellow eyes, and a ridiculous-looking thin black plume that dangles behind it like a bad fashion choice. Palm fronds rattle in the gentle breeze. Several white ibis peck with their long curved bills in the lawn of the small bungalow across the street, snapping up bugs. Spanish moss hangs limply from the live oak in the parking lot. Brown lizards skitter, dashing like streakers on a dare across a crowded street.

Finally, a shiny black sedan pulls up and the lawyer, a dusky-skinned Indian woman, steps out, juggling a briefcase, a travel coffee mug, various folders and a purse. She walks around the car and up the path and smiles at me as she unlocks the front doors.

"Good morning," she says with a cheerful smile. "I wondered if I would see you today. Happy birthday."

"Thanks," I say. "You're the first to wish me that."

"Then I'm honored," she says. She holds the door open for me and I step into the cool, dark office. She flicks on the lights and offers me coffee or tea, which I refuse, too anxious for any delays. Sensing my impatience, she heads past the empty reception area and into her office, motioning for me to follow.

"Now, then," she says, settling behind her neat and tidy desk. "I imagine you have some big plans. How can I help you?"

"I have an account to close out." The blood roars in my ears.

She's clearly disappointed, but maybe not really surprised. I listen to a dull speech about the advantages of saving money, the amazing benefits of IRAs and the power of annuities. Wise advice that amounts to: please don't blow all your money.

I let her finish and then hand her a slip of paper with Isakson's account information. I give her my instructions and then add one more task.

"Do you know a good tax attorney?" I ask.

She smiles faintly and nods. "I know the person you need to speak with."

If I had a million dollars sitting in a trust fund, thinks Lavanya Sarin, I simply would not disperse it all on my birthday, certainly not my eighteenth birthday.

Lavanya watches the girl leave the office, mount her bicycle and ride away. She wonders what sort of parents let a young child control so much money. Why did they not advise her about the precariousness of the future? Why did they not tell her that when you are young, you cannot comprehend the needs of your future self, the capriciousness of future events? Certainly, she should be allowed to spend some of it, certainly. But all? In one morning?

She shakes her head in bafflement and sips the sweet, spicy chai in her travel mug. She has lived in this country since she was eighteen, but her parents' strong, wise influence has helped her see past the desire for instant gratification that colors the younger generation of Americans. Hard work, sacrifice, dedication, family loyalty. These are the values that make a happy life.

She thinks about her twins, almost six, and as studious and anxious to please as she was so many years ago. They will grow to be proper adults. Respectful, hardworking and wise. She is fond of Lenore Kohn and thought her a clever girl, but there's no denying her actions today are puzzling in the extreme. She thinks of her parents back in India and how much she misses them. They visit every year and she has visited twice with the twins, but nothing compares with the joy of having parents living nearby. They considered applying for a green card and emigrating, but they would not qualify for Medicare and are not eligible for Social Security. They simply could not afford to live in America and therefore, their family is split apart by thousands of miles and nine time zones. How sad that so many Americans do not appreciate their great fortune to be born and raised in this land of possibilities.

Though there are no clients in the office and no meetings sched-
uled until after lunch, there is much for Lavanya to do. She forces
her brain to cease its melancholy musings and turn to the matters
at hand. There is almost nothing a neat and orderly mind cannot
achieve.

It's nearly ten when I arrive at Professor Isakson's office. The
money is already wired to the start-up's account. It's done.
There's nothing left for me to do except watch how it all comes
together. Or falls apart.

The professor lets me in.

"Did he come?" I ask.

Isakson shakes his head. He looks like he wants to say something, but then changes his mind.

"It's early yet. Give him time."

I follow him into the extra office. There's a pot of brewed
coffee.

"You'll have a cup?" he asks in an awkward, well-meaning
way. My second offer of the morning.

"I'd love one," I say gratefully. "Thanks."

"You are my great benefactor. The least I can do is offer you
a cup of coffee."

So he checked his account balance. I feel a sudden rush. I
gave this man a million dollars! The fact that he knows somehow has made it all real.

"You never really believed me, did you?" I can't help gloat-
ing a little.

"You'll forgive me, I hope," he says. "I don't often find myself living in a fairy tale." He hands me a cup of steaming black coffee. "Cream? Sugar?"

"Both," I say. It could be a long day. This might be the best moment in it. I should celebrate.

I feel light and clean, a little giddy. This must be what the frog prince felt like when he finally became a human again. The curse has been lifted, and I too feel like a human again. I can't stop smiling. We clink mugs and I propose a toast.

"To the future of your company and making the world a better place."

"To AlgaeGo," he seconds, and we drink to seal the toast.

"About that name," I say as we sit down to wait for Gavin. "I've been thinking . . ."

We discuss the merits of various names. He insists it's too late for a new name since there's already valuable name recognition, while I maintain that there's always room for improvement.

Time passes. The banter peters out. I send up a little prayer that Gavin is okay and that he'll be here soon. Isakson rises frequently from his seat to search the sidewalks visible from his third-story window, glancing at his computer and, clearly, wishing he could do something about all the work that needs to be done.

"It could be a long day," I say. "Feel free to work on whatever you need."

To show him that I mean it, I tuck my legs under me and check my phone, which keeps chiming with incoming happy birthday texts. I skim each one but none are from Gavin. Deleting the latest text, I catch Isakson looking at me, shaking his head.

"I . . . ," he begins, then shakes his head again. "I have been a professor for a long time and I have met many students. Some were brilliant. Most were plodding, unoriginal thinkers who were self-involved and self-centered. It's natural, you understand. I'm not judging," he says, catching my raised eyebrow. "It's human nature." He touches his beard, almost petting his own chin, an unconscious gesture that I've noticed he makes when he's searching for words. "But this—I have never even heard of someone your age doing this. This is the work of an old person, ready to leave the world, wanting to leave a legacy." Given his awkward ways, I forgot how brilliant the professor's mind is, or how subtly it can work. "I don't understand how you can do this."

"I've always been mature for my age," I joke. He doesn't smile as he studies me with his hooded eyes, waiting for a better answer.

"Your reasons are your own," he says. "You certainly have earned the right to be private, but I have learned a little about your family situation and the news this morning of the fire at your sister's shop. . . ." He spreads his arms in helpless confusion. "In light of that, I find that I don't understand your actions at all."

My shoulders tense at the mention. I really wish he hadn't done his homework. The silence stretches uncomfortably for a while until I can't bear it.

"It wasn't our money," I finally blurt out. "It wasn't our money in the first place. I needed to give it away. Give it to someone who can really use it and spend it in a way that might help fix some of what's broken."

"You mean because you won the lottery, you didn't earn the money?"

"Something like that."

"There are more worthy organizations," he points out. "I am not running a charity. And I might be out of business by next month."

"Notice you're saying this after the money's in your account," I tease.

He smiles but doesn't leap to defend himself.

I squirm in my seat, wondering how to explain this in a way that someone as brilliant and subtle as the professor will be satisfied. "Your situation gave me a chance to buy two priceless opportunities simultaneously. No one gets 'accidentally' accused of cheating. It was a deliberate, malicious effort to sabotage the course of Gavin's life. I have a chance to undo that and help out your potentially world-changing company at the same time." *I hope . . .* Though I don't say that part out loud. "Am I making a mistake?" I muse out loud for his benefit. "I hope not. But it was the only thing I could think of."

This doesn't make sense to the professor.

"I'm not going to ask for a refund," I say to his unvoiced concern. "No matter what happens today. If Gavin comes or not. If he turns in crap or gold, the money is yours and I hope that you'll spend it better than the rest of my family did. And if I've leveled the playing field against that awful Professor Parks, well, that's something too."

He processes everything, reading between the lines, behind them, before finally nodding in politeness, if not true understanding.

But I told him the truth—no matter what happens, I don't regret giving Isakson the money. It's also true, though, that there's a big difference between prolonging the death knell of his company and shooting it off in the right direction to create renewable energy while putting Gavin back on track.

As the day progresses, my shoulders tighten in knots, the headache growing between my eyebrows pulsing like a beacon. As I stretch my legs, the blood rushes in painful prickles.

Maybe the devil didn't need to mess with me at the attorney's office. Maybe there was an easier target out there, a target he's already nailed. Like Gavin crossing a busy street, tired and distracted. Or maybe the fact that I'm leaving my parents destitute makes things perfectly fine with him. Maybe he's laughing so hard right now, he's pissing in those sexy jeans Natasha liked so much.

We call in a lunch order, from a nearby deli that delivers.

"My treat," he says. "I insist."

Since I'm now officially broke, I let him. Though I'm hungry, the sandwich is tasteless and the grilled portobello mushroom feels like rubber in my mouth. I push it aside after only a few bites.

That morning coffee really was the highlight of my day.

At four in the afternoon, I begin to fear that Gavin isn't coming. Maybe there was traffic on I-75. Maybe the sites didn't work out. Or the landowner didn't want to negotiate.

I'm as tired as if I've been working in the hot sun all day, drained, wrung dry, yet twitchy. Too much coffee, too much sitting. My cell phone is full of texts and missed calls. Several are from Natasha but until I have something to report, I'm not answering her calls.

My bottom is numb from sitting so long, my legs achy, and my morale very low. Even after six hours of waiting, I haven't fully lost faith that he will show, but the doubts are getting more insistent.

Depression sets in. Isakson will look at Gavin's proposal no matter when he turns it in (if he turns it in) but I also know that Isakson's heart, while kind, works in partnership with his mind—which is cynical and judgmental. By placing Gavin under such a tight deadline, I set him up for failure. Isakson is going to deem him a slacker, unable to turn in an assignment on time.

I walk over to the window and look out at the dismal little street the building faces. There's a homeless man sleeping in a stripe of shadow against the building.

Traffic on the road thickens, the start of rush hour. A small section of the I-275 overpass is visible from the office, and while traffic is moving, it's slower now than it was a couple of hours ago. I lean my forearm against the hot windowpane and rest my forehead on my arm.

A flock of roseate spoonbills, ridiculously pink, flying in V-formation, pass by the building, almost at eye level with me on the third floor. I watch them flit by, and smile despite my terrible disappointment. Their spoon-shaped bills, combined with their pink feathers, always remind me of characters from a Dr. Seuss book. They fly above the street, heading to some swampy pond.

That's when I see him, a small figure jogging down the sidewalk. He's two blocks away, but there's no way I'd ever mistake that tall, loping form.

I gasp and spin away from the window.

Isakson rises, his face lightening.

"He's here," I say.

"Come, come," Isakson urges. We talked about this earlier. He opens a closet door and I step inside. The door has slats, so I can see the room.

Isakson hurries back to his desk and rearranges papers, striving for a casual, why-no-I-wasn't-expecting-anyone look. The door to the office suite creaks as it opens.

"Hello?" Gavin calls out. "Anyone here? Professor Isakson?"

"In here!" the professor calls out, in a pitch-perfect tone of irritated surprise, though I hear the undercurrent of nervous excitement.

Gavin enters the room, staggering a little and bumping into the door on his way in. He's uncoordinated, awkward on his feet. His face is haggard and he looks years older. *Gavin, don't sleep, if that's what it takes,* I said to him and that's what he did. His hair is lanky and greasy. I am humbled, amazed at what he's put himself through. Because I asked him to.

Isakson rises and comes around the desk to stand near Gavin. He's much shorter than Gavin, yet he seems to loom over him.

"Please, sit down." The professor gestures to the chair where

I've spent the entire day. Hopefully, Gavin doesn't notice it's body-heat warm. "What can I do for you today?"

Gavin sits, his big hands braced on his knees, his posture straight as he prepares to present his case. My arms are covered in a wave of goose bumps as I'm suddenly transported in time to two and a half years ago, watching his trial as he sat behind the defendant's table, wearing a suit for the first time, a carefully blank face to try to hide his thoughts, though his fear and tension were clear.

"I—um—I . . ." He fumbles for words. "I have—I mean, I came up with a business model. I think you'll be interested." He rubs his forehead hard, as if trying to press the right words out of his exhausted brain. It hurts to see this. Gavin, who talks fast and thinks faster, can barely get a straight sentence out. I clench my fists by my sides, willing him to keep it together, to hang on and get through this. Without saying anything, the professor hands him a bottle of water. Gavin cracks the seal and drinks deeply. When he starts talking again, his voice is less crackly.

"I remembered back at Tech, you told us about your company, AlgaeGo," he says. "That was last year and ever since then, I've had this idea. . . ." Gavin fades off. It might be my imagination, but it seems that Isakson gets a smug little smile at the mention of his company name. He shoots a glance toward the closet where I'm hiding that seems to say: *Not such a bad name after all, is it?*

"Yes?" He turns back to Gavin.

"Um . . ." Gavin, who unconsciously followed Isakson's gaze

to the closet, shakes his head. "Sorry, I lost my train of thought." He fires up his laptop, clicks on a few icons and then turns it around so that it faces the professor.

The two of them hunch over it and Gavin explains how leasing the land will bring the trials of algae/fuel production out of the lab and into the world. That investors like to see progress, not perfection. Then he lays out the (very favorable) terms of the lease that he negotiated on behalf of the company. I can't see the screen, but some information appears that makes the professor lean forward in sudden attention. The polite interest is gone. Isakson asks some questions and Gavin runs a different model to illustrate his point.

"It's good," Isakson says, ever the master of the understatement.

I have to stuff my fist in my mouth to keep from shouting and jumping up and down with triumph.

"I'll pay you for the work." He names a huge sum that makes my eyes pop open. But Gavin has barely heard him. He's already shaking his head.

"No, no, I'm not selling it."

"What do you mean?" Isakson crosses his arms in ire. "Then why did you come here?"

"I'm giving it to you."

Professor Isakson drops his arms in dumbfounded shock. But he quickly recovers. A cynical look crosses his face.

"You think I'll give you a job? Get you reinstated at Tech?"

"If you hire me, that would be amazing, a dream come true," Gavin says. He has bruise-colored bags under his eyes.

He stands up for his last rebuttal. "But the truth is, I'll work for free. I'll make coffee. I'll take out the trash. I was willing to pay thirty thousand dollars a year to go to college for one class a semester with you. I'd be willing to pay a lot more to work with you full-time."

"Sit down, Gavin," the professor tells him. He's trying hard to maintain his poker face but for once everything he's feeling is visible and I swallow hard at the answering emotions that clog my throat. "Tell me what happened to you at Tech. Tell me all of it."

I hear it again, straight from Gavin to his hero. And he's so tired that he can't mask the hurt and the confusion about what was done to him.

"And the worst part of it is that I feel like you left Tech because of me. Like I drove you away."

Isakson shakes his head.

"I miss the energy and the optimism of my students. It wasn't an easy decision to leave Tech but no, my boy, you did not drive me away. It was time for me to go. My company was growing too fast for me to keep teaching. It was the right time for me to move on." He places a kind hand on Gavin's shoulder, who seems to relax with sudden absolution. "Perhaps it worked out for the best that you are no longer at Tech. I would be honored if you became a partner at this company."

Gavin grins and much of the strain on his face is gone. He still looks exhausted, but also years younger than he did when he first walked into the room. "Thank you, sir."

"Stay right there," the professor says, patting Gavin's shoulder. "Let me pull up some paperwork and we can make this official."

He leaves the room and Gavin leans forward, resting his head on the edge of the desk. It's only when the professor comes in and Gavin doesn't sit up that I realize that he's out, sound asleep.

The professor falters for a moment when he sees Gavin slumped over, and then pats him, very gently, before turning to my hiding place.

I rush out of the closet and hug the professor.

"Thank you, Professor Isakson," I whisper, feeling a giddy rush of excitement. "That was amazing. It was worth every penny."

He hugs me back, a great, tight hug. "I don't say this a lot," he says. "But I was wrong. Thank you for making me reevaluate."

I grin, too full to speak.

"And please," he adds with a little smile, "call me Tovar."

Chapter Twenty-Three

The house is warm with bodies and candles. There's music, something Caribbean with a great beat. There are carafes of tropical iced tea, platters with small appetizers, and napkins with a palm-tree design, my name and today's date embossed on them. My mother must have worked like mad to arrange everything so quickly. No one would be able to tell this was a last-minute switch or that this morning she was up to her ankles in soot and ashes, wading through the ruins of the tea shop.

Someone shrieks my name and everyone turns to look at me. Hands reach out for me, pulling me this way and that. Faces blur in a wash of wide-open eyes and moving lips; I can't make out the words. Someone steps on my foot. I jerk at the sudden pain in my toe and end up head-butting someone leaning in for a hug. Then my mom grabs my arm and pulls me out of the cluster to the counter and shouts for attention.

"Leni is here, everyone! Time to sing Happy Birthday. Ready? One! Two! Three!" The crowd gamely begins to sing, low and off-key. I stand there, squirming from all the attention. Trying to be gracious about this. Trying to be grateful.

When they finish on a long, warbling note, I smile and clap.

"Thanks, guys," I say loudly. "Nice singing." There are some chuckles. "Thank you for coming, enjoy the party!"

They clap for me and then, thankfully, I'm out of the spotlight. A few well-wishers seek me but the intense attention quickly passes and soon I'm watching guests have fun at my party, as removed from them as if I were standing across the street watching them through the windows.

My parents have been swept up in their host duties and are chatting with old friends. There haven't been this many people in our house since the year we moved in, when my parents held a huge housewarming party.

It takes what feels like eons to make it to my parents, like I'm wading through Jell-O. Who knows what platitudes come out of my mouth or who I'm talking to. As I get close to them, someone grabs my hand. I turn, annoyed, but when I see who it is, my face softens.

"Eddie." My voice lilts in surprise. I expected him to hole up in his room until the crush passed.

He's perched uncomfortably on a stool against the wall, wearing a clean black shirt and jeans that squeeze his wide thighs. He's sweating from the heat and probably from the overwhelming press of people after months of self-imposed, nearly solitary confinement.

"It's your birthday, kid, the big one-eight. What kind of brother skips that?"

"It would have been okay," I say softly. "I would have understood. Besides, I thought you were mad at me."

"I don't know if 'mad' sums it up. 'Enraged,' 'appalled,' those come a little closer."

I stiffen. "Fine, why did you come, then? I did what I said, so if you came here hoping that I didn't—"

"It's okay, Leni."

I blink and raise my eyebrows.

"Yeah," he says to my unvoiced question. "Really. I'm okay with it. I thought a lot about what you said. There's a part of me that's been waiting all this time for someone to come hand me another chunk of change. And when I finally realized that wasn't going to happen, I also realized that it's a stupid thing to wish for. My baby sister is giving her money away to someone she thinks deserves it—though I have to tell you, kid, I still think you could have done better than that jackass—but regardless, I realized that if my own sister wasn't going to hand it over to me, or even to Mom and Dad, well, maybe it's because we don't deserve it, you know? We don't need it. And then I realized that I've wasted half of my twenties. I mean, what the heck? It doesn't get any better than this. I have to rescue my own fat ass. No one is going to do it for me."

I blink faster, trying not to cry.

"Eddie, that's fantastic."

"It's like the fog burned off, you know? I feel like it's the first time my brain is working since I got back from Bali."

I hug him, tightly. He hesitates for a moment and then gently wraps his big arms around me. "Not that Mom and Dad necessarily see it that way," he warns.

"I know," I say. "I'm about to tell them."

"Good luck."

"Yeah, I'm going to need it."

"Leni," he says as I turn to go.

"What?"

"It was a good decision. I'm proud of you, sis."

"Thanks." I smile. "That means a lot coming from you."

When I finally make it to my parents, I wait as they finish their conversation. I catch something about a sailing trip and calling to firm up plans later next week. I swallow past the lump in my throat.

"Hey, Mom, Dad," I finally interrupt. "This is a great party. You did an amazing job."

My parents turn with a glad smile and I'm enveloped in their arms and their familiar, comforting smell. I soak up the feeling of their strong arms around me. This is my childhood. This feeling of love and security, the certainty that everything will be okay because my parents are here.

When I finally step away from the hug, I step away from my childhood. I'm eighteen and a lot has changed since yesterday.

My mom is high from the social success of the evening. It couldn't have been easy to switch venues on the fly and yet she pulled it off. The pleasure from her success has taken years off her face. She looks truly happy.

"I gave away my money this morning," I say.

My mom doesn't hear me at first. It's loud in here—the background music with its pumping beat is barely audible over the roaring conversations of the guests. It's my dad that gets it. His jaw slackens and his lips tremble before he presses them tightly together.

"Mom." I keep going, knowing I have to make her understand. "I gave away my trust fund. All of it."

She hears me this time, but it takes her a minute to process the words. She's looking at me, with all the love shining, and then, slowly, there's a furrowed brow, a math equation with the answer out of reach. Then a little half smile—it's a joke, right? Except she sees my serious face, anxious and guilty, and she turns to my dad.

"Did you . . ." She sees that he already understands what she's starting to figure out. "Did you know about this?" she asks in a strangled voice.

"No," he says. "No, I didn't know." I can hear in his voice what he doesn't say out loud. How could I *not* have told him?

They both turn to me and for a moment they look alike. Then I realize it's that they both have the same sucker-punched expression on their faces.

I clutch my hands together. "I'm sorry I'm telling you this way. I know this isn't the time and I really wish I could have told you earlier. But I'm not sorry that I did it."

"You're not sorry you did this?" my mom says, turning white with rage.

"I shouldn't have done it as a surprise. I was afraid that you'd stop me and . . ."

My dad looks like he's fighting tears.

"How could you do this?" my mom hisses. "Do you have any idea what you've done? Do you think money is only about trips? About clothes? Money is about never being hungry or cold. It's about taking care of each other. You didn't even ask! You didn't even give us a warning!" And then she wails, "I'm going to look like a fool!"

"I love you," I say, fighting to keep my voice steady. "I love you so much, but winning the lottery was the worst thing that ever happened to our family. I want my family back. I don't want fancy lessons or trips. I don't want a wasted brother or a crazy sister. I want my family." I swipe at my tears. "I hate our horrible house. I hate your fake friends who like you when you spend money and don't call you back when you're broke. I hate that you and Dad stopped working at the shop together. We had a good life!" I don't know if the guests can hear this. I don't care. "That money was cursed, you know it was! It bought us nothing good."

My mom won't look at me.

"I'm sorry, Mom," I whisper. "I didn't want to hurt you."

"Can you undo it?" she suddenly asks, her eyes blazing with some nameless mania. "You can still get it back, right?" She twists my arm. Her manicured nails, a vivid burgundy, dig into my skin enough to make tears of pain well in my eyes, this from a woman who never raised a hand to me in anger my whole life. She doesn't even realize she's hurting me. She doesn't care.

"No." I shake my head, eyes wide to keep the tears at bay.

This is going about as badly as it could go. "No, Mom, I can't get the money back. It's gone forever."

"Who was it? Who did you give it to?" she hisses, spraying my face with spittle. "I can make them give it back. You're young, you don't know what you're doing. Tell me who you gave it to!"

"This is why I didn't tell you what I was going to do," I burst out, jerking my arm out of her grip. "I knew it would be like this!" I rub my sore arm, feeling little half-moon indentations left by her nails. "I'm not telling you." I shake my head. "The money is gone. It's not coming back." With a cry of disgust, my mom turns, pushing me away in a throwing motion, as if she's getting rid of me. She wedges herself against the wall with her back to my dad and me, hands covering her face as her whole body shakes with sobs.

I look at my dad, afraid of what I'm going to see on his face.

But he's not crying or looking at me in disgust. There's something in his gaze that makes me think maybe he understands.

My mom pushes past us, heading to the bathroom to fix her face. A few people turn their heads to watch her fly by. Rumors will not be far behind.

"Dad?"

"Lenore," he says gruffly. "I always knew you had a will of iron behind that sweet, quiet face."

"Are you furious?" Of course he's furious. What did I think would happen?

"I'm not going to tell you this is a pleasant announcement," he says. "And I sure wish you had picked a different way to break the news." He gives me a stern look. "You ruined your mother's evening and she worked very hard to give you a beautiful party."

I nod, my eyes downcast.

"But when we gave each of you a trust fund, we gave it to you. It means you get to decide. Not saying it'd be my first choice, but then again . . ." He shrugs. "Life is full of surprises, I guess." Then with something close to the old twinkle in his eye, he winks at me. "It might be interesting to go back to the old shop."

I smile tentatively.

"You still love me?" I ask, rubbing the sore spot on my arm, feeling frozen inside.

"Of course I do, Leni," he says in fond exasperation, warming my frozen core. "And so does your mother. Give her a day to recover from the shock, and we'll all sit down together and see where we stand." He pulls me into a big hug.

"We are a great family and great families adjust," he says firmly, kissing the top of my head. "Have a little faith."

Chapter Twenty-Four

No one shouts goodbye or *Leaving so soon?* as I slip out of the house as quietly as I entered. Which goes to show this party was never about me. I amble down the packed driveway, cars parked every which way, and I'm crossing the street when someone calls me. I turn, expecting to see someone from the party, but instead Gavin hurries to catch up.

"I didn't want to crash the party of the year," he says. "But I have something for the birthday girl."

The nap he's had clearly did him good, though his face still has lines of fatigue and there are heavy bags under his eyes. He reaches into his pocket and hands me a small gift-wrapped box, no bigger than a matchbox.

A tiny pair of rose-petal tellin shells, smaller than my pinkie

nail, nestle inside. They look like miniature butterfly wings, the exact color of the sky at twilight. There's a small drop of silver soldering to strengthen the point where they connect and a small loop so that they can hang from the thin silver chain.

"I found the shells during the beach cleanup. I picked them up and then I saw you fall. I don't know why, but it seemed like it was something you should have."

As I cup them gently in my hand, I realize that they look like a pair of tiny angel wings.

Wordlessly, I hand him the necklace and turn, lifting my hair so that he can fasten it around my neck.

I touch the shells. They feel cool against my skin.

"It's perfect," I say. "Just perfect."

I glance over my shoulder at the lit house, scanning the milling crowd through the windows until I find my dad. He's holding my mom's hand, talking earnestly and gesturing with his free hand as she listens, her head bent to catch his words. He's animated, rising several times to his toes, perhaps painting some lovely picture of the future. Maybe it isn't surprising that my dad recovered first. Perhaps all that money never sat right with him either.

"The bioluminescent plankton are in," Gavin tells me, drawing my attention away from the party. "The bay is glowing green and blue. It looks like there're thousands of tiny LED lights underwater."

"Really?" I ask, pulled from my turbulent thoughts in a manner I didn't think was possible on this night. "I missed seeing them last year."

"So come see them now," Gavin says, with a grin at the look on my face. He reaches for my hand and I gladly take it.

"You seemed kind of distracted and upset last week," he says. "You good now?"

"I will be," I say. "How did your trip down south go?"

"It was way more complicated than I expected. But I saw Isakson this afternoon," he says. "Kohn, you'll never believe it. He hired me on the spot!"

Somebody on the sidewalk behind us starts to whistle a bright little tune.

We walk along a streetlamp-lit path that is as straight and true as a compass line. Ahead of us lies a glowing ocean, teeming with the promise of endless possibilities.

He watches them go with a sneer on his striking, charismatic face. Some of the writhing, wretched fury that he always carries with him leaks through, and he knows this. He has to be careful. He quickly schools his features back to their standard operating mask.

You win some, you lose some. He's been around long enough to know that, though he never plays to lose, damn it, and he really thought he had a winner this time. Gavin walking away was a year's work lost. His eyes glint red as his rage flashes. It seemed foolproof when Gavin was expelled from school.

He shrugs, shaking off the loss. You move on to bigger and better things. He has more than a couple of projects running that he has high hopes for. Delicious, really, all these plump little chickens running around.

There's a lot of potential with Jennifer and Drew, their musk of

desperation so strong he wouldn't have to dangle much to get them to jump on board.

Joanie was dim and callow, but she was so eaten up with envy that he knew from experience there were great possibilities there.

Captain Homeless had slipped his grasp. But there were more. Always more. Plenty who thought their lives were worthless and that they didn't have anything to lose. Plenty who were barely hanging on. One more setback. One more plan gone wrong and they were his for the taking. Everyone has their vulnerabilities. And you never knew what was waiting around the corner.

He chuckles to himself. Most of the time, he's the nightmare waiting around the corner.

The thought cheers him up considerably.

Remembering that there's no time like the present, he heads off to check on his latest pet—the lawyer who misses her parents— whistling a happy tune.

Chapter Twenty-Five

Three months later, the investigation into the tea-shop fire closes. The fire marshal rules it arson and charges are filed against my sister. Other than one eyewitness saying she thinks she saw three people in the shop, there's no evidence that any-one was in the shop other than Natasha when the fire started. And everyone knows that eyewitness accounts are remarkably unreliable. Natasha's been assigned a public defender.

It turns out that John Parker had been skimming from the profits for months, but when my sister started falling apart, he saw an opportunity to increase his revenue stream. He falsified order forms, emptied the store's accounts and fled the state. If I still had my million, I would bet every single cent of it that John Parker started the fire. But as far as anyone can tell, he's fallen off the face of the map. The defense attorney is planning to blame the fire on the disgruntled, thieving ex-employee, but at the end of the day, the only person who would gain from the fire was my sister.

Seven years after winning $22 million, the five of us Kohns are back in the old house, in the old neighborhood, in our old rooms, Natasha and I in bunk beds, Eddie barely fitting on the couch since his old room has been turned into an office for the company.

The big mansion sold at auction for a fraction of what was owed on back taxes and the mortgage. But my parents were allowed to leave without being responsible for the difference and in the end, they were grateful for that. An anonymous benefactor paid off all the back taxes on the old house. My parents often wondered which of their wealthy friends was behind the kindness or whether it was one of the many unfortunate souls they'd helped along the way, paying back a moral debt. It eased them, thinking of all the possibilities, feeling that someone was looking out for them. Someone was.

I sent off my application to Stanford and indicated I would need financial aid. I expect to hear back sometime next month. After that, who knows? I applied to a couple of state schools as well.

My parents changed their voicemail message. It now says: *You've reached Kohn's Electrical. We're out with another client right now, but we'll call you back as soon as we're able. Thanks for calling!* My mom's voice at her most chipper. They don't have that many clients, actually, but the *Tampa Bay Times* recently wrote a story about the lottery winners who lost their house and returned to their old line of work. Business has picked up since they ran the piece.

I can't say that things are amazing. Money is tight. I didn't realize it but we were living off food-bank donations for months at the big house and my mom still swings by once a month for several bags of groceries. We need the help. So we eat Golden Puffs cereal instead of granola, Great Value "red sauce" instead of marinara, canned green beans instead of fresh, and we're grateful to have them.

But in a lot of ways, life *is* better. Eddie enrolled at SHCC. He wants to learn AC work and add a cooling/heating division to Kohn's Electrical.

My sister is a mess. She wears baggy jeans and old T-shirts from the shop. She never laughs, hardly eats or sleeps. I miss my sister who was confident and sexy and ready to take on the world. It hurts me to look at this ghost that drifts through the house. She lost the shop and she lost Emmett, the two things she hoped to gain with the lottery win. She also lost a lot that she never bargained for, but I can't stop thinking about what she's done and wondering if she will ever forgive herself for whatever it was. She still refuses to speak of it. I don't think she's planning to fight the arson charges very hard. Part of her clearly wants to be punished, even if it isn't for the crime she committed.

Gavin is a partner with AlgaeGo. He's completely broke, since he and Tovar are reinvesting every penny they've got into making the company grow. But the company is solvent and their future is bright. *Scientific American* is writing a piece about them and there is major interest in their research from a Japanese firm. It isn't always easy working for Tovar, but Gavin says he's learned more in three months with AlgaeGo than he possibly could have in four years at Tech. I keep telling them both they should change the name. So far, I've been overruled. EarthFuel is still nipping at their heels. But with the first batch of algae happily burbling away in South Florida, Tovar and Gavin feel confident as to who will finish first.

I returned the beach cruiser my parents bought me for my birthday. My dad found a couple of rusted bikes on the curb on Big Trash Day and he began tinkering. The frame on one of them was solid, the pedals on the other were still okay. It inspired him to troll through town and soon he had five bent and broken bikes to pull parts from. He salvaged enough working parts to put together one working bike. It's a Frankenstein sort of bike, but it works. I ride it to school, to SHCC and to our favorite ice cream shop. It's no sweet beach cruiser, but Eddie spray-painted it sky blue and Gavin scored little green fish decals at a convention that I stuck all over it, and even Natasha pitched in, donating the wicker basket that connects on the front. Let's just say it'll be a hard bike to steal since it's rather bizarre and highly recognizable.

I wear the shell necklace every day and it reminds me that there's beauty and mystery in this world, in the least of places, on the most ordinary of days.

Michael has not returned. But I know he's out there. They all are.

I lift the shells and touch them to my lips. They're warm

from my skin. I step up onto my bike and start pedaling to school.

It's a gorgeous Florida winter morning. There's a cool nip in the air that will mellow into a balmy seventy degrees by the afternoon. The citrus trees in the neighborhood are heavy with bright globes of sweet oranges and peach-colored grapefruits. A thin little black racer sunning itself on the driveway quickly slithers away at the sound of my approach, slipping over the ground like a shadow. A huge airplane full of tourists roars overhead as it comes in for a landing at the St. Pete/Clearwater airport. As I'm looking up at the plane, an osprey flaps its powerful wings, clutching a good-sized fish in its talons.

Ospreys are terrific hunters, yet they were almost wiped out back when my parents were growing up. DDT, the popular agricultural insecticide that helped control mosquitoes, caused their eggshells to be too thin and they would crack before the chicks could hatch. After DDT was banned, ospreys slowly began their comeback and now they are almost as common as squirrels. Meaningful changes can happen. Big problems can be fixed.

I drop my necklace and it settles back in place just below the dip of my collarbone. I stand on the pedals and pump harder, knowing I only have fifteen minutes to get to school and loving the whoosh of wind, the feeling of flying.

An endangered wood stork, startled by my passing, awkwardly flaps its large black-tipped white wings and takes off.

I am eighteen.

It's a lucky number in Judaism. It symbolizes life.

* * *

Lenore sails past him on her bike, hope and happiness streaming behind her like the banners medieval knights used to fly. She doesn't notice him. No one ever does unless he means for them to see.

There are other people he needs to keep an eye on. Yet he cannot tear himself away from Lenore. It's her joy, her optimism, that he finds so lovely. He closes his eyes and feels her happiness on his skin. He can taste it. And he knows he needs to savor it, to make it last.

Not all his stories have happy endings. There's a family in Nashville that will never be the same. He needs to work on that. There's a troubled young man there who might be able to help them.

It's time to move on. Angels are forbidden to contact their charges without proper authorization. It's only when Asmodeus begins the meddling that he's allowed to come in, for balance. There will not be another visit to Lenore, he knows this.

But he also knows that she's carved a place for herself in his heart. All his charges do. Though she will never see him again, he will be with her always.

Michael gathers himself to leave, steeling himself for his next task. There are two young children whose mother is about to make a very wrong choice. They will need him to help them through the coming crises.

God speed you, Lenore, he whispers to the wind and then he becomes part of it, blowing by.

An endangered wood stork, startled by the sudden gust, awkwardly flaps its large black-tipped white wings and takes off.

259

Acknowledgments

Writing this novel took a lot of help from a lot of talented, kind people before it became what you're reading today. In no particular order, I deeply thank Jeremy L. Balsbaugh of Hunt Laboratory, at the University of Virginia Department of Chemistry; firefighter David M. Frost, of the Hillandale Volunteer Fire Department, Montgomery County Fire and Rescue Service; Battalion Chief Paul Atwater, Seattle Fire Department; Assistant State Attorney Tony Julian, Juvenile Division Chief Patti Pieri, and the Hillsborough County State Attorney's Office, Juvenile Division; Rabbi Danielle Upbin; marine scientist and Antarctic explorer Paul Suprenand; Gabriel, Aharon, and Dan Laufer, a trio of savvy businessmen who made AlgaeGo possible; my fantastic agent, Stephen Barbara; Katie Hamblin of Foundry, a keen, subtle, and fast reader who came to my rescue; and my talented editor, Erin Clarke, and the rest of the wonderful staff at Knopf. A special thank-you to Professor Joan Kaywell, of the University of South Florida, who does more for YA writers in general—and Florida writers (and readers) in particular—than anyone I've ever met, and who did so much to welcome me to the Tampa Bay book-lovers community. Fred, my first reader, my biggest fan, none of this would work without you. Tovar and Delaney, who remind me what's really important, and here's a hint: it doesn't have anything to do with winning Powerball.

Tammar Stein is the author of the young adult novels *Kindred, High Dive,* and *Light Years,* which was an ALA-YALSA Best Book for Young Adults, a Virginia Readers' Choice, and a Texas Tayshas High School Reading List Selection. She lives in Florida with her family and a bilingual dog. Visit her at tammarstein.com.